NAME
UPON
NAME

About the Author

Sheena Wilkinson is the award-winning writer of a number of books for young people. She lives in County Down.

Other books by Sheena Wilkinson
published by Little Island

Still Falling (YA)
Published in spring 2015

Too Many Ponies (children's)
Shortlisted for CBI awards 2014

Grounded (YA)
CBI Book of the Year 2013
CBI Children's Choice 2013

Taking Flight (YA)
CBI Honour for Fiction 2011
CBI Children's Choice 2011

NAME UPON NAME

Sheena Wilkinson

Little Island

NAME UPON NAME

First published in 2015 by
Little Island Books
7 Kenilworth Park
Dublin 6W, Ireland

ISBN: 978-1-910411-36-0

A British Library Cataloguing in Publication record
for this book is available from the British Library

Cover illustration by Niall McCormack
Insides designed and typeset by Oldtown
Printed in Poland by Drukarnia Skleniarz

Little Island receives financial assistance from
The Arts Council/An Chomhairle Ealaíon
and the Arts Council of Northern Ireland

10 9 8 7 6 5 4 3 2

Too long a sacrifice
Can make a stone of the heart.
O when may it suffice?
That is Heaven's part, our part
To murmur name upon name,
As a mother names her child
When sleep at last has come
On limbs that had run wild.

from 'Easter 1916' by WB Yeats

For Susanne Brownlie
with love and thanks for many years of friendship,
in and out of books

Acknowledgements

Thanks to Siobhán Parkinson and Gráinne Clear for giving me the opportunity to write *Name Upon Name* and for being so enthusiastic about the project. I love historical fiction and have always wanted to write a book set in this period.

Thanks to Briege Stitt in the Local Collection of Downpatrick Library for her help in tracking down helpful books for research. Susanne Brownlie was a tireless supporter of *Name Upon Name* from the start: thanks for reading, commenting and most of all for liking Helen and her family so much. Likewise, huge thanks to Julie McDonald who read the book with a historian's eye. Many years ago, Alison Jordan, my history teacher at Victoria College, Belfast, inspired me to love history. I wish she were still alive: I know she'd be delighted that I grew up to write a book set in 1916.

Writing this novel was very intense: more thanks even than usual are due to my family and friends for keeping me fed, entertained and reasonably sane. My wonderful agent, Faith O'Grady, is a constant source of wisdom, and as always has been there to support me throughout. Fellow writerly folk, on- and offline, you know who you are, and I hope you know how valuable it is to be able to talk to you.

During the revising of this novel, I was fortunate enough to spend a week in the magical surroundings of the Tyrone Guthrie Centre at Annaghmakerrig. More than for any previous book, I know its unique atmosphere helped to make Helen's story come alive to me.

And finally, but perhaps most importantly, thanks to everyone who reads my books, especially when they go to the trouble of telling other people about them. I hope you enjoy this latest story.

Historical Note

This novel is set mostly in Belfast in the early part of 1916. At that time, all of Ireland was part of the United Kingdom. Ireland was represented by MPs (Members of Parliament) who sat in the British parliament in Westminster in London.

Some Irish people (mostly Catholics) were Nationalists. That meant that they did not want to be part of the United Kingdom but wanted to have a separate Irish state. Other people (most of them Protestants) were Unionists, and they believed that Ireland and Britain belong together and wanted Ireland to remain British. Most of the Unionists lived in Ulster.

Home Rule was a kind of compromise solution. Home Rule would mean that Ireland could have some independence and its own parliament in Dublin, but that Ireland would still be part of the United Kingdom, and the British parliament would still have power over Ireland in some respects. Many Nationalists, including John Redmond, leader of the most popular Irish political party, supported Home Rule, but others felt it did not go far enough; and of course the Unionists were against it, because they wanted Ireland to remain British.

Home Rule for Ireland was just about to be brought in, when war broke out between Britain and Germany. This war (later called World War I) started in 1914 and did not come to an end until 1918. Many battles were fought in northern France and in the area of Belgium called Flanders. It was a terrible, terrible war and millions of young men died horribly in it.

Irishmen from Unionist families were often very keen to join the army and go to war; Irishmen from Nationalist families had more mixed feelings. Redmond believed that if Irishmen joined up that would help Britain to win the war quickly, and then, when things got back to normal, Home Rule would come in. Other Nationalists felt that joining the army and helping the British was not the right thing for Irishmen to do if they wanted an independent Ireland.

Some Nationalists believed that the only way to get Irish independence was to have a rebellion (or a rising) against British rule. And they felt that this was a good time to rebel, because Britain was busy fighting in Europe. The 1916 Rising took place on Easter Monday, mostly in Dublin, led by Patrick Pearse and James Connolly among others. The rebellion was quickly quashed by the British, the leaders were executed as traitors and Britain continued to wage war in Europe for another two years. Home Rule for Ireland never did come in, but eventually the Republic of Ireland was set up as an independent state and Northern Ireland remained part of the United Kingdom.

These were dreadful times for both Nationalists and Unionists, Protestants and Catholics, and especially for the men killed and wounded in battle and their families. The characters in this story are caught up in these conflicts, they have different religious and political loyalties, and the story shows how historical events reach into the lives also of the people who do not fight – mostly the women and children – as well as those who do, and can tear families apart with grief, loss and bitterness.

LITTLE ISLAND

JANUARY 1916

1.

'Saint Anthony will find your brooch for you – he's the patron saint of lost things. Just say a wee prayer.' As soon as the words were out of Helen's mouth, she knew she'd made one of her blunders.

Aunt Violet pursed her lips and sat up even straighter on the settee. 'There'll be no need for that, thank you.' She didn't say 'Catholic nonsense' but Helen imagined the words hovering in the air around them, in Aunt Violet's parlour, which was usually chilly but had a cheerful fire today in honour of 1916 being only two days old.

Her cousin Sandy winked at her, and Helen tried not to giggle – no point in giving Aunt Violet more reason to find fault with her. But as she bit back the giggle, she felt a little bubble of happiness. When Sandy had first come home from the war in France he would never have winked like that. He was obviously better, but that meant he would be leaving soon. People were always leaving.

As if she could read Helen's thoughts, Aunt Violet, in her smoothest voice, said, 'It's a pity your poor mother won't be home for your birthday tomorrow.' She accepted a teacup from Granny.

Granny answered because Helen had a mouthful of tea-loaf. 'Sure it's worth it if that country air makes her chest better.'

Helen's legs felt prickly on the horsehair sofa, even through her petticoat and thick woollen frock. Without ever directly criticising Mama, Aunt Violet always seemed to be saying more than her actual words. Helen had once overheard her saying to a friend about Mama, 'A very nice woman in her way, but you know, they Aren't Like Us.' 'They' meant Catholics. 'Your poor mother' indeed! As if Mama wanted to be ill so often!

Papa and Helen didn't really like Mama spending so much time at Derryward, her brother's farm in County Down, but they muddled along without her when they had to. Helen knew she ought to be sorry not to be going to visit Mama on her birthday, but she'd much rather spend the last few days of Sandy's leave with him. He'd be going back into danger soon enough. She sighed.

Sandy gave her a little poke in the arm. 'You'll blow the fire out, puffing like that,' he said.

'Och, she's disappointed not to have her mother on her birthday,' Granny said, as if Helen were turning four, not fourteen.

Helen was about to protest, but it was easier to say yes than to tell the truth. 'Well, a bit,' she said. 'But it's silly to mind something so small when there's a war on.'

'I don't think people stop minding things just because of the war,' Sandy said.

'But it seems so *childish*.'

'You *are* a child.' Sandy sounded amused.

Helen burned with indignation, but if she wasn't a child then *what* was she? A young lady? She didn't fancy having to be proper all the time and give up reading school stories, and wear longer skirts.

'Why can't you go and visit her?' Sandy asked. 'Term doesn't start until Wednesday.'

'Papa's school starts tomorrow, though,' Helen explained. 'And *he* can't really take a day off, being the headmaster.'

'And there's nobody else to take you?'

Helen shook her head. Even if she'd been sixteen or eighteen or even *twenty* she wouldn't be allowed to take the train so far by herself.

Sandy thought for a moment, and ran a hand through his ginger hair. The scar that puckered his skin from elbow to wrist was faded to a purplish line.

'I'll take you,' he said. He raised his voice. 'Ma?'

'Sandy, don't call me Ma!' Aunt Violet said.

Sandy grinned. *'Mother,'* he said, 'I'm taking Helen to see Aunt Eileen tomorrow. For her birthday.'

Granny clasped her hands together. 'Oh, what a kind thought!' She beamed at Helen.

Aunt Violet did not beam. 'Are you sure that's wise, son? It's such a long journey, and you on sick leave.'

'If I'm fit to go back to active service on Thursday, I think I can manage a wee jaunt down the country.'

Aunt Violet sucked in her lips as if to stop them bursting out a protest. Helen felt a tiny twist of sympathy. *She* didn't want Sandy to go back to the Front either, but you couldn't say that. It was hard enough for the boys out in France without their womenfolk going mushy on them. And Aunt Violet was proud of Sandy. He'd got his commission in the army as soon as he left school. She'd never have wanted him *not* to do his duty.

'I'd have thought you'd want to spend your last few days at home with your family,' Aunt Violet said.

'Helen *is* my family,' Sandy said, and Helen glowed.

Sandy had been head of house at school and captain of the first fifteen: she'd loved the glory of being 'Sandy Reid's little cousin'. Even still, older pupils stopped her in the corridor to ask how Sandy was getting on. And now – to have Sandy and Derryward *together* seemed the most glorious thing that could happen.

'You could come too, Aunt Violet,' she suggested, safe in the knowledge that Aunt Violet's list of reasons not to go to Derryward was a long one. 'I'm sure Aunt Bridie would make you very welcome.'

She tried to imagine Aunt Violet in the big, cosy farmhouse with its rows of woolly socks warming above the range, and sometimes an orphan lamb wrapped in an old sack. Aunt Violet might – just – have coped with socks and livestock, but she would never have been able to sit in the same room as the Sacred Heart picture. Even Helen's cousin Michael's silver cups for Gaelic games – he was a brilliant hurler – would have made her lips disappear inside her mouth with disapproval. She wondered what Sandy would think – Sandy had won plenty of cups too, but his were for cricket and rugby. It would be the first time her boy cousins had met. The two halves of her family, Reids and O'Hares, had never had much in common.

Swallowing the last of her tea-loaf, Helen had a sudden cold fear that Sandy and Michael, probably her two favourite people in the world, would hate each other.

2.

Helen swung her legs against the stone wall behind the farmhouse and cuddled a kitten for warmth. She watched the boys below her in the yard, Sandy helping Michael fix some wooden palings into a pen for an injured calf. They hunched over their task, Michael's tweed cap beside Sandy's grey one, Sandy broad-shouldered, Michael wiry, hands working deftly, the smoke from their cigarettes drifting into the chill January air like their conversation. Fly the sheepdog stuck close to Michael's legs, retreating to her kennel by the wall when there was any hammering being done.

From where Helen sat, she couldn't hear their words but she knew what they were talking about: war war war. She'd stuck it for ages, but in the end a mixture of boredom – Michael wanted to know about the dullest things – and fear – that Sandy would reveal something horrible – had driven her off in search of other amusement and she had found the tabby kitten with the scratched nose. Of course it was wonderful that Sandy and Michael had taken to each other so well; it was stupid of her to feel left out.

And after all, she was meant to be here to see Mama. But Mama said the wind was too cold for her to be outside, and Helen couldn't bear to stuff indoors. She ruffled the tabby kitten's soft fur, and breathed in the clear mountain air that was so sweet after sooty Belfast. Even the air in the park opposite her home never felt as crisp and clean as it did in Derryward. She was sure it would do Sandy good, stocking up on that good County Down air before he went back to France.

'What are you sulking about?'

She turned to see her cousin Nora carrying a basket of eggs, her dark hair pulled back into a plaited bun as if she were grown up. At school, only the sixth form girls wore their hair up. Nora was fifteen and had left school. She helped Aunt Bridie with the poultry and the garden, and she could already cook a dinner for the whole family. Helen immediately felt that her own two plaits were little-girlish.

'Not sulking. Just – I wanted to show Sandy round the farm. But now he's busy helping Michael.'

'Well, they're boys, aren't they?' Nora shrugged. 'Bound to want to stick together.'

'They're talking about the war,' Helen said. 'Michael wants to know all about it.'

Nora set her egg basket down carefully on the mossy ground and leant against the wall. She had a proper bosom and her tweed skirt was much longer than Helen's.

'I wish they wouldn't.' She frowned. 'The last thing we need is a British soldier putting ideas in Michael's stupid head. He and Daddy fight enough as it is.'

'Why?'

'Michael has this insane idea about joining up.' Nora sounded contemptuous. 'And obviously Daddy's raging.'

'Why?'

Nora sighed, as if Helen were very stupid. 'It's England's quarrel, not ours.'

'But we're *part* of –'

'Not for much longer.'

'You mean Home Rule?' Helen tried to sound knowledgeable. Everyone she knew – apart from her mother's family – was against Irish Home Rule. Her father and Sandy's father, who was dead now, had queued for hours in 1912 to sign the Ulster Covenant, pledging to keep Ulster British.

'Yes.' Nora sounded very confident. 'Ireland won't bear the yoke of tyranny for much longer.' She said these words as if she was reciting a poem. 'But Daddy, and Gerry, who works for us' – she blushed – 'and any Irish person *worthy of the name*' – she looked at Helen as if she were a very nasty sort of insect – 'say we should take advantage of England being at war to fight for it *now*.' Her dark eyes gleamed.

Helen shivered. She'd grown up closing her ears to adults prophesying war on the streets of Belfast over Home Rule. Now there *was* a war, and it was a hateful one, but at least it was far away in France and Flanders and the Dardanelles. It was all very well for Nora to sound so careless: there'd never be violence here, in these quiet green hills.

'*I* think,' Helen began – and realised that she wasn't sure *what* she thought, except that inside her was still a small girl clapping her hands over her ears – 'that's *mean*. Like taking advantage of someone when they're down.' She thought of all the talk at school about fair play and playing the game. 'It's – it's unsporting,' she said. There was nothing worse you could be at Belfast Collegiate than unsporting. 'Ungentlemanly.'

Nora laughed, but not merrily. '*Ungentlemanly*.' She imitated Helen's accent. 'You even *sound* British.' She made it into an insult.

'I *am*. So are you.' Dislike of Nora's smugness made Helen more confident than usual. 'Ireland is British, whether you want it to be or not. Whatever Uncle Sean says. And he's only a *farmer* – *my* father's a teacher and *he* says –'

'I'm *not* British. I'm Irish and I'd die before I'd be anything else. *You* don't know what you're talking about.' Nora's cheeks flamed; for a moment Helen thought she was going to hit her. But Nora simply pursed her lips, bent down to lift the eggs, and stomped off down the hill to the back door, swinging the basket.

The kitten mewled and struggled and, when Helen made a grab for it, shot out a tiny paw and scratched her hand. She dropped it, and it scampered off under the spiky whin hedge, tiny tail aloft with injured dignity. Helen sucked her hand, annoyed at the tears pricking the backs of her eyes. She didn't even *like* Nora much, so why was she upset at fighting with her? 'You don't know what you're talking about.' As if Helen were a child.

But maybe she was? She *didn't* know – or care – much about Home Rule, and being Irish or British. She just knew she hated people talking about it. She had always quite liked having the excuse that she could see both sides because of Mama and Papa being from different religions. But maybe that was just laziness? Maybe she ought to be able to make up her mind?

Still, what was the point? She brushed the kitten's hairs off her coat. Adults would sort it out – *men* would sort it out

– and whatever happened Helen would just carry on living in Cyclamen Terrace beside the park, going to school and playing hockey and being best friends with Mabel. She'd go to church with Papa as usual on Sundays, while Mama went alone to mass in the big convent on the main road.

She scrambled down from the wall and set off to join the boys.

'That'll do now,' Michael was saying, looking at the newly-made pen. 'We'll set it up in the corner of the barn, if you don't mind helping me to carry it in?'

He straightened up and pressed his hands into the small of his back. Fly, thinking this was a game, barked and jumped up, leaving muddy paw-prints on his trousers.

Sandy flexed the fingers of his bad arm. His cheeks were reddened with effort and with the January air.

'Just give me a minute before I lift anything. It's fine but it hasn't been put to the test much until today. Smoke?'

He pulled out a packet of Gallahers, offered it to Michael, and then, obviously joking, to Helen in the kind of gesture that might have delighted a seven-year-old.

Helen tossed her plaits. 'Don't be silly,' she said. 'Michael, is it true that you want to join up? But Uncle Sean's against it?'

Michael's eyes widened in surprise, as if a kitten had started talking.

'But if you're a Nationalist, do you not hate England?' she went on.

'Not *hate*. It shouldn't be ruling Ireland,' Michael said. 'And it won't be for much longer. But I *do* hate sitting round on the farm doing nothing when other lads are joining up.'

His dark eyes, exactly like Mama's, were restless.

'You're not *doing nothing*,' Sandy said, his Belfast accent contrasting with Michael's softer one. 'And even if conscription comes in – farmers will be exempt.'

'There'll be no conscription in Ireland,' Michael said, in the same confident way that Nora had said Home Rule would come. 'That's the surest way to start a rebellion.'

Rebellion? Helen shuddered. *But I'm not a baby,* she thought, *I'm fourteen; if I were at Papa's school I'd be leaving now and going to work, so I should know things. I'm not a little girl to tease.*

'So – Uncle Sean thinks there should be some kind of rebellion?' she made herself ask. 'While the war's still on? But you – don't?'

'Da and Gerry say Ireland never got anything off England except by violence.' Michael drew on his cigarette. 'I want an Irish Ireland and I'll fight for it if I have to.' He looked across the yard at the hills, and the mountains in the distance. 'But helping England win the war is the surest way to get it.'

'Sure that's what Redmond's been saying since the start,' Sandy said. 'That's why he's been encouraging Nationalists to join up. And plenty have. Out there – well …' He stubbed out his cigarette under his boot.

'Ready?' he said, nodding at the palings. The boys bent and lifted them, and carried them into the barn together, Fly darting importantly ahead.

Helen ran to help and, though the wooden palings were heavier than she thought and the boys didn't really need her, she made herself bear some of the weight.

3.

It wasn't the best birthday tea Helen had ever had, despite the beautiful cake Aunt Bridie had made, with fourteen pink candles.

Partly it was worry about Mama. Despite having rested most of the afternoon, she seemed tired and ate little, crumbling a scone in her long thin fingers and breaking off every so often to cough into her handkerchief. Helen wished Mama was strong and rosy like her sister-in-law. Mama was pretty but she didn't do many of the things other mothers did. Even at home she spent long hours reading, or just lying on the *chaise longue*, not knitting or sewing – 'Just being,' she'd say when Helen would come in from school and ask what she was doing.

Now she removed herself from the tea-table – they always sat round the table for tea at Derryward, in the bright parlour whose window looked straight across to the Mourne mountains, which Helen much preferred to the balancing acts she had to perform with plate and cup at Aunt Violet's. 'I don't want my cough to annoy people,' she said.

'Go and sit by the fire, Eileen,' Aunt Bridie said.

'But come back for me blowing out my candles?' Helen could have bitten her tongue – there she went again, sounding like a child.

She caught Nora's scornful dark eyes and looked down at her plate. She and Nora Weren't Speaking, but she didn't think anyone had noticed. And Nora might have

29

called Sandy *a British soldier* in that rude, unwelcoming way, but it didn't stop her from being enchanted by him, fussing round him, refreshing his teacup when it was still almost full.

Helen heard the click of the back door latch. Aunt Bridie's broad face broke into a smile. 'There's your Uncle Sean at last,' she said.

Uncle Sean was huge and red. It was hard to think that he was Mama's brother. His loud voice – 'I defy any cattle to break through that fence now' – preceded him into the room, followed by his woollen-jerseyed belly and finally his big roughened face.

He nodded at Helen. 'Happy birthday, daughter,' he said. He always called her daughter. He called all girls daughter. 'What are you now – ten?'

Helen swelled with indignation and then realised he was joking. 'Ninety-three,' she replied with dignity.

He gave a snort of laughter. 'Is there tay in that pot, Nora?'

He noticed Sandy for the first time and nodded.

Sandy swallowed his last crumb of soda bread and stood up to shake Uncle Sean's hand. 'How do you do, sir?' he asked. 'I'm Helen's cousin, Sandy Reid.'

'You're welcome here.' Uncle Sean looked Sandy up and down, as if assessing him as a possible worker. Helen felt proud: Sandy was nearly as tall as Uncle Sean, and even though he wasn't in uniform he looked, in her eyes, every inch the young officer. No wonder Nora was gazing at him with her big bovine eyes.

'Thank you, sir,' Sandy said.

'Michael – have you that job finished?'

Michael nodded. 'All set up in the corner of the barn and I've the calf moved in and all. He's well settled.'

Helen thought of the scruffy brown calf, its cut leg smeared in some kind of purple lotion, and how trustingly it had lain in Michael's arms before he had set it gently into its pen.

Uncle Sean grunted. 'Did you give him plenty of hay?'

'I know how to look after a calf.'

The edge to Michael's voice made Helen look up in surprise: she had never heard it before.

'Bloody nuisance, getting himself cut like that. And me and Gerry wasting a whole day fixing the fences.'

'It's the barbed wire,' Michael said. 'I keep telling you.'

Uncle Sean stared at him over the rim of his cup. 'Barbed wire's saved me a fortune. Never mind the time it takes to mend walls.'

'The dry-stone walls are beautiful, though, sir,' Sandy said. 'I haven't been to this part of the country before and they were one of the first things I noticed. It must be a skilled job.'

'Aye, it is. And half the men in the country away. Bloody fools.'

'No, they're not,' Michael said. He frowned at his plate.

'Don't *start*,' Aunt Bridie said. 'Not when we've a guest. And it's wee Helen's birthday.'

Nora smirked at the 'wee Helen' and then, probably trying to sound grown-up in front of Sandy, said in a put-on, showy-off voice, 'I suppose you must see a lot of barbed wire at the Front? I've heard it can do terrible damage?'

The air seemed to shudder. Sandy shook his head, his cheeks suddenly white under his freckles, his blue eyes darkened with something Helen couldn't read – a memory? She knew the injury to his arm had been caused by ripping it on barbed wire while he'd been trying to get one of his injured men back to safety. The man had died of his wounds. Sandy had never told her this, but she had overheard her parents talking.

I hate you, Nora, Helen thought. She might only be fourteen today and she didn't have much of a bosom yet, and childish plaits and short skirts, but for goodness sake! *She* knew better than to talk about wire, or trenches, or people being killed. Especially when Sandy was going back in two days' time.

'Isn't it time for my candles?' she said loudly, and Nora tossed her head and rolled her eyes, but Sandy gave Helen a tight, grateful smile.

Helen lit the fourteen pink candles with one match and everyone cheered. But she wasn't sure what to wish for – there were so many *big* things this year. She could wish for Sandy to stay safe; for Mama to get better; for there not to be any kind of rebellion or trouble. She closed her eyes, inhaled, felt the heat of the candles caress her cheeks and decided just to let the wish come to her.

She exhaled.

I wish I could be more grown-up.

There was clapping, and when she opened her eyes she saw she'd managed to blow out every single candle.

4.

'No, Michael, I'll take them.' Uncle Sean heaved his bulk up from his chair. 'I don't like you driving in the dark. You go too fast. You'll have the mare wore out.'

Michael sighed and made as if to protest, but Aunt Bridie reached over and squeezed the top of his arm, as if to say, *Don't argue.* Helen wanted to say they could walk to the station, but it was too far. For the first time she was happy to leave Derryward. The tension between Uncle Sean and Michael made her feel hot and prickly.

Mama kissed her and hugged Sandy and wished him well; Aunt Bridie gave her some of the cake, wrapped in greaseproof paper; Nora muttered goodbye, not looking up from her crochet; and Michael said that she could take the tabby kitten for a birthday present. Helen looked hopefully at Mama but Mama shook her head.

'I can't have cats in the house,' she said. 'They make me cough.'

'Sure it'd stay outside,' Michael said.

At Derryward the cats were never in the house, roaming the outhouses and getting fat on mice.

'There isn't anywhere outside,' Helen said. 'Only a tiny front garden and a back yard.'

Michael shook his head as if he couldn't imagine this. He had never visited Cyclamen Terrace. He had once been to Belfast for a hurling match, but that had been over the other side of the city.

Outside, the lichen on the stone walls gleamed in the moonlight, and the mare's breath was a frosty cloud. Helen sat in the back of the trap and looked at the broad tweed backs of Uncle Sean and Sandy in front. The chill evening air scratched her cheeks.

She tried to block out the conversation – more boring politics. She would have called it an argument except that Sandy was being very calm and kept calling Uncle Sean 'sir'.

Uncle Sean said, 'Yous boys have had it all your own way for centuries. But yous can't hold back the tide now. Home Rule's coming one way or another.'

'I hope not, sir,' Sandy said. 'But if it does there'll be special provision for Ulster. Ulstermen won't stand for a Catholic state.'

'And Irishmen won't stand for a divided country.'

Men, Helen thought, *always men. Irishmen. Ulstermen.*

She wished she hadn't squandered her birthday wish so foolishly – all she longed for now was for them to be at the station before Uncle Sean flew into one of his rages. But he didn't. He clicked his tongue and the mare trotted faster. They were on the main road now, and as the trap swung uphill to the wayside station the ring of her iron-shod hooves was the only sound in the darkness.

In the train, they had a compartment to themselves. It might get busy after Ballynahinch, but for now Helen lolled in her seat in a way that would have outraged Mama and Aunt Violet. The drumlins of County Down, black humps in the moonlight, sped past the windows. It was hard to believe that tomorrow morning she would be sitting in Latin class and giggling with her best friend Mabel Craig and helping make up parcels for the former pupils at the Front – old boys' parcels, they called them. And soon Sandy would *be* at the Front. She sighed and dug her hands deeper into her coat pockets. Sandy pulled one of her plaits and drew her into a sideways hug.

'Tired?' he asked.

'Yes,' she began, then, remembering her wish, 'no, of course not.' It was lovely, slumping against Sandy like this, feeling the rough wool of his overcoat against her cheek, and he must have quite liked it too because he didn't move away.

'It was funny, seeing Aunt Eileen there,' he said. 'She seemed more comfortable than she does at home. I suppose it's where she grew up.'

Helen bit her lip.

'Sorry,' Sandy said. 'Was that the wrong thing to say? I just meant – well, it's good that she can go there. For her health.'

'Hmmm.' Helen didn't want to talk about Mama.

Sandy looked at her keenly. 'Talking of saying the wrong thing,' he said, 'thanks for – you know.'

Helen did know. 'Nora's a beast,' she said. '*And* she has a pash on you. She couldn't keep her eyes off you!'

'Well – dashing young officer. It's understandable.' He grinned, but then lapsed into one of his old silences. The train trundled on through the black evening. People got on at Ballynahinch but nobody came into their carriage.

'You didn't mind talking to *Michael* about the war,' Helen said, when the train got going again.

'Not really, no.'

'Because he's a boy?'

'I suppose so. He reminded me of the boys in my platoon.' He looked out of the window, and said, in a casual tone, 'I wonder how many of those boys are still alive.'

Helen had a quick fantasy in which Michael joined up and ended up in Sandy's platoon, and they would save each other's lives and get medals, then both come home and be safe forever. She shook her head at her own idiocy. If Michael did join up – and of course he wouldn't, Uncle Sean would kill him before the Germans did – even *she* knew that Catholics and Protestants tended to join different regiments. *If I were a boy,* she thought, *which one would I join? Because I'm neither one thing nor the other. Maybe neither would want me.*

'I'm glad I'm not a boy,' she said.

Sandy didn't reply. Helen gave him a tiny kick – as always when she had been at Derryward, her boots were dusty, with a rim of dried mud. Some of it broke off and fell on to the wooden floor of the train. 'Sandy?' she said. 'I may not be a boy but I'm not a *child.*'

'What do you mean?'

'You could tell me things.'

He sighed. 'Better not. It's a different world. People can't understand.'

'Not if you don't tell them the truth.'

'Do you really think my mother wants to know the *truth*?'

'She reads us your letters.' Sandy's letters – longed for, celebrated, but always, secretly, for Helen, rather empty. He had said more in the letter he'd sent to the school to thank them for his old boys' parcel. 'You always say everything's fine.'

'That's what she wants to hear. It's like – well, like you not wanting to talk about Aunt Eileen.'

For a moment Helen felt bruised, and then it was a sudden relief to say, 'I know she isn't happy. We all say it's her chest, but it's more than that.'

He took her hand and didn't let go. His felt rough, the skin drier than her own.

'You're not "wee Helen" any more, are you?' he said, looking at her closely.

She met his blue eyes with confidence. 'No, she said, 'I'm not. And I don't mind hearing nasty things. If anything ever happens that you want to tell someone – you can write to me. I won't tell anyone.'

'Promise?'

Helen nodded and squeezed his hand. 'Promise,' she said. And wasn't sure whether she should hope for such a letter, or pray that Sandy would never need to write one.

5.

When Miss Linden wasn't at prayers, and then didn't show up for history first lesson, there was a lot of gossip in the lower fourth. At least, the girls gossiped; the boys, on their side of the classroom, lounged against desks and wondered if the pitches would be too hard for rugby this afternoon.

'Maybe she got married and left,' suggested Florence Bell.

'She probably has flu,' Mabel said. Florence's notions were not to be encouraged, and Helen and Mabel spent a great deal of time avoiding her – she lived in the same street as Mabel. 'I had it the whole holidays. I couldn't eat a *thing* on Christmas Day.'

Mabel looked fine now, her face as round as ever, her dark curls already springing out of the velvet band that was supposed to keep them off her face. Looking at those curls, Helen touched her own hair self-consciously. She had experimented with one plait today, tying it top and bottom with navy ribbon. It *felt* secure enough, but she had no idea what it looked like.

'Mabs,' she whispered. 'Will you check my hair's all right at the back?'

Mabel spun her round, pronounced the single plait 'very swish' and said, 'She can't have got married, Florrie – her fiancé's at the Front.'

'Maybe he got Christmas leave?' Florence couldn't bear to give up on a romantic story. 'Or maybe she ran off and married someone else.'

'Maybe she married Peg Leg!' All the girls collapsed at the idea, and then, as if they'd conjured him up, Peg Leg himself, moulting books and paper, shuffled into the room.

'Ladies! Gentlemen! To your places *at once*.'

The boys folded themselves into their desks more noisily than they needed to, and even the girls, who thought themselves above such behaviour, didn't stop their giggling and whispering as quickly as they would have done for any other teacher.

Peg Leg – Mr Perry to his face – had lost a leg at Neuve Chapelle, and been invalided home. Dr Allen had given him the job because so many of the regular masters had joined up, and Perry was an old Collegian, with a brilliant degree from Queen's University, but he was even more unpopular than old Mullan, dragged out of retirement to teach Latin, or Miss Thomas, who policed the girls for Unladylike Behaviour.

Perry had been a lieutenant, same as Sandy, but while Helen could easily imagine Sandy leading men into battle, she couldn't think of Perry as anything other than shrill and ineffectual. 'Shell-shocked' was Florence's diagnosis, and 'mutilated, poor man'. She tried to make Perry a romantic figure, but he was so irritable, and given to doling out punishment lessons – 'just for *breathing*', as Fred Morgan complained – that she wasn't very successful. Even so, Florence made a point of ostentatious raptness in Perry's classes, while chaos reigned around her. Helen didn't see Perry as remotely romantic: his blotchy face would blush redder and redder as the boys banged their desk lids, or pretended not to hear his orders, or, at a signal from Fred Morgan, dropped their books all at once.

Today Perry tripped a little, stepping on to the teacher's dais, and dropped a sheaf of essays. Florence, beaming with virtue, leapt forward to gather them up.

George Rae, who was usually top of the class, raised his hand. 'Sir, we were expecting Miss Linden now.'

'Yes,' Perry said, in the reedy voice Helen couldn't imagine giving orders. 'I'm afraid Miss Linden will not be with us for some days. Her brother has been killed. Naturally Miss Linden is comforting her parents.'

For the first time in one of Perry's classes, the lower fourth was silent and remained so for the whole lesson.

★★★

Helen and Mabel pushed open the storeroom door at the start of break. The room, always hot from the boiler room next door, was extra stuffy after being shut up for the holidays, and Mabel at once broke into a fit of coughing.

'It's the dust,' she gasped, when Miss Cassidy, who was in charge of the old boys' parcels, looked concerned. 'I'll be fine in a minute.'

But when Miss Cassidy heard that Mabel had just recovered from flu, she sent her outside for fresh air. Which was typical of her; she was easily the kindest of the teachers. Helen was tempted to go too – something about the old boys' parcels always made her feel sad – but it was her turn to help, and that was that. It was Florence's turn

40

too, but Florence had cried so much about Miss Linden's brother – not that she'd known until today that Miss Linden *had* a brother – that she'd been sent to Matron to lie down.

After the holiday, the central table was piled high with khaki socks and mufflers, tins of sweets and cigarettes and a few cakes. The shelves were stacked with brown paper and string. It was amazing, Helen thought, that all these parcels, made up in odd spare moments, should actually make it out to the Front. She checked the list pinned to the wall – four sheets of foolscap paper; name upon name of former Belfast Collegians – some long left school, others, like Sandy, only recently. When one was killed, Miss Cassidy always put a neat black cross against his name. She never crossed the name out.

Helen bent over her work, sorting the woollens into piles. They were all shades of khaki – the wool shops in Belfast must be doing a roaring trade in dull khaki wool. Perhaps a soldier at the Front would welcome red or yellow socks for a change. Socks, muffler, gloves, gloves, socks – oh dear, what scratchy wool; no soldier would want to march with those on his feet. Sandy had had his parcel in September, just before he was wounded. She wondered where he would be by the time it was his turn again. He was leaving tomorrow. Socks, muffler –

'You're very quiet today, Helen,' Miss Cassidy said. 'Good holiday?'

Helen nodded. 'I got all Jane Austen's novels for Christmas,' she said.

'Wonderful. Have you read them yet?'

'Started,' Helen said. She had also had some school stories, and she'd devoured those, but she knew Miss Cassidy wouldn't be impressed by *The Girls of the Hamlet Club*. She was Helen's favourite teacher – she often asked about Sandy, and she always gave Helen good parts to read when they did Shakespeare – but she was quite serious.

'If you're going to go to college,' Miss Cassidy said, 'it's never too early to start reading properly.'

'*College*?'

'Why not? It's 1916. Lots of girls go to college now. You know that. And you're one of our brightest girls.'

'I can't be!' Helen burst out. Her voice sounded loud and high in the tiny room; she clutched a soft muffler to her front. 'I mean, I know I get good marks but how can I be bright when I don't *understand* anything?'

Very much to her own surprise, she found herself telling Miss Cassidy some of the thoughts that had been buzzing round her head since yesterday. She couldn't discuss them with Papa; he was too certain about everything. And Mabel would only say it was daft to worry about things like politics and beliefs. But Miss Cassidy listened as closely as if Helen had been explaining her thoughts about Lady Macbeth or the poetry of Keats.

'And I don't know *what* I think, or *who's* right,' Helen said. 'I suppose I've always just agreed with Papa. Or' – because it somehow mattered to be very truthful – 'I suppose I haven't really bothered thinking about it much at all. I don't know if I feel British, or Irish – I think I'm *both*, but I don't suppose that's even allowed.'

42

'Well …' Miss Cassidy considered this, her eyes thoughtful behind her spectacles. 'At least you get to think things out for yourself, don't you?' She said it as if that was simple; as if it was a good thing.

'But everyone seems to have a *side*. I don't have a side. I'm just …' She chewed her bottom lip and started back on her sorting. Socks, gloves, socks –

'Just what?'

'Scared,' she admitted.

'That's all right,' Miss Cassidy said.

'It's not, though, is it? Not in wartime. *Sandy*'s not scared. At least – maybe he is, but he's still doing his duty.'

Miss Cassidy smiled. 'I think Sandy feels very clear about what his duty *is*. That's bound to make it easier. And from what I remember' – she had taught Sandy for three years – 'he's more of a doer than a thinker. You're obviously a thinker.'

Helen had never considered herself a thinker. A worrier, maybe, but a *thinker*? She added a packet of Gallahers cigarettes to the socks and sweets in her first parcel.

'This war won't last for ever,' Miss Cassidy said. 'But it *will* change the world – and for the better, I hope. Especially for women. You need to be ready to take your place.'

Again she made it sound very simple. And really quite exciting. Which it might be for someone who knew what her place was.

6.

As soon as Helen stepped into the hall, she knew that Mama was home. Mama's scent – lilac and rose and something delicate and elusive that was just Mama – was all around, and Mama's blue coat hung on the coat rack. Helen tossed her satchel on to the ground, where Papa was bound to fall over it when he came home, and ran into the parlour, the unfamiliar heavy plait bouncing on her back.

'Mama?'

Mama was at the window, running her finger along the sill. 'I think Mrs Magee has been taking advantage,' she said, showing Helen the thin layer of grey dust on her white finger. 'But it's so hard to get anyone to help in the house these days. Helen – that tunic! It barely reaches your knees!'

'I've grown,' Helen said, as if she hadn't seen Mama for months, instead of less than twenty-four hours ago. 'Mama – why are you home?'

'Aren't you pleased to see me?'

'Of course!' She rubbed her face against her mother's shoulder. 'I'm sure you shouldn't be messing around with dust.'

Mama laughed. 'Maybe not.'

She sank down into one of the armchairs beside the fireplace. The grate was empty, because Helen and Papa always sat in the back room, which was a little shabby but much cosier.

'I'll set a fire for you,' Helen said. 'Mrs Magee would've done it if she'd known –'

'It doesn't matter.'

Helen sat in the other chair, but she couldn't sit still, leaping up to show Mama her new hairstyle, and then to look at the new green brooch Mama wore on her cream high-necked blouse, a Christmas present from Aunt Bridie. It was a little shamrock in chips of Connemara marble, much prettier than the sapphire brooch Aunt Violet had kicked up such a fuss about.

Papa was as surprised as Helen to see Mama. 'You didn't even send a wire,' he said, shaking his grey head. Papa was much older than Mama.

'So does this mean you're better?' Helen asked. Mama hadn't been better yesterday – she had been tired and she'd coughed by the fire during the birthday tea. How could she be recovered enough in one day to brave the grimy Belfast streets? Had she missed Helen and Papa too much to stay away?

'I'm all right,' Mama said, though she suppressed a cough and frowned. 'I just wanted the peace of my own home. Michael and Sean had a terrible row last night. Poor Bridie's heart is broken. And it brought it all back to me –'

'A row? About Michael joining up? Best thing he could do,' Papa said. 'If I'd a son …'

'Be thankful you haven't.' Mama sighed. 'Sean sees it as a betrayal of his culture. And I know how he feels.'

Helen normally shut her ears to this kind of adult conversation, which she classified as *boring, with the potential to get worrying.* And that cryptic remark of Mama's – 'I know how he feels' – that was about Helen going to the Presbyterian church; Mama never came out and said she hated it, but they all knew she did. But remembering her birthday vow, she said, 'Didn't Mr Redmond say Nationalists *should* fight?'

Again, that surprised look, as if a kitten had spoken, but Papa smiled and said, 'Glad those school fees are going to good use.'

'I didn't learn it at school,' she said. 'Sandy and Michael –'

'Please.' Mama clenched her fists at her sides. 'No political talk. I've had enough of it at Derryward. Mostly shouting.'

She frowned at her reflection in the over-mantel mirror. 'I don't know how it will end,' she said. 'Bridie's terrified of what they could do to each other. Son against father.' She shuddered.

Helen wondered what she had meant by 'It brought it all back to me.' She knew both families had been against her parents' marriage.

'I must speak to Mrs Magee,' Mama said.

Helen and Papa exchanged glances and then followed her down the tiled passage to the kitchen, where, as usual, their daily help Mrs Magee had left a cold supper. She lifted the white cloth and poked at the cold meat and bread. *If I were Nora*, Helen thought, *I could have had a hot dinner on the table for us all.*

'Since when did Mrs Magee leave so early?' Mama asked. 'She's supposed to stay and feed you.'

'Since her son came home from hospital,' Helen said. 'He can't do much for himself, and she worries about leaving him for too long.'

'You see?' Mama said to Papa. 'Be glad you have a daughter. Whatever worry she causes you, she won't have to go and get maimed in some war.'

'Helen's never caused us any worry,' Papa said, pulling the end of Helen's plait.

The gesture reminded Helen of Sandy. He was leaving in less than twenty-four hours.

'She'll cause us enough when she starts falling in love,' Mama said. She lowered her voice, as if she didn't want Helen to hear. 'Bridie doesn't know what to do about Nora. She's far too great with that Gerry. And he seems a bit of a hothead. Has her head filled with romantic notions about Ireland.'

Helen winced. 'Maybe I'll never fall in love,' she said. She thought of that surprising conversation in the storeroom. 'Maybe I'll be a blue-stocking like Miss Cassidy and go to college.'

Being like Miss Cassidy was a much more attractive prospect than having her head 'filled with romantic notions', like Nora.

'Miss Cassidy?' Mama opened her eyes very wide. 'That strident young woman we met at the Red Cross fête? I hope *she's* not the kind of woman you admire? You'll be saying you want the vote next!'

'Well, maybe I do,' Helen said. Though who would she vote for?

Mama sighed. 'After last night,' she said, 'I'd be much

happier talking about something gentler. Why don't you read to us, James? Or play the gramophone?'

'We might as well eat now,' Papa said. 'And then – well, Helen usually has prep for school, and I have paperwork to do. I'm sorry, Eileen. If we'd known you were coming …'

'I do live here.'

'Of course.' Papa touched Mama's shining hair. 'And we've missed you. We'll have a wee celebration tomorrow.'

'Sandy leaves tomorrow,' Helen said. 'We may not feel much like celebrating.'

7.

Of course they all *felt* like crying, standing in the draughty station at Queen's Quay. But they didn't, though Helen bit the insides of her cheeks so hard that tears of pain sprang to her eyes anyway. Sandy was leaving alone this time, so in a way it was worse than the first time, when the station had been crammed with soldiers and well-wishers. Before anyone knew what it was like out there.

'I'm only going as far as London,' Sandy reminded his womenfolk, which, today, included Mama. He looked tall and unfamiliar in his uniform – a brand-new one. 'A course for two weeks before I get anywhere near a sniff of action. So don't start worrying yet.' He grinned.

The whistle shrilled – and he was gone.

In the darkening street outside, they looked at each other.

Mama was first to speak. 'Come back to our house for a bit of supper,' she said to Aunt Violet and Granny. 'James will be home soon; he'd love to see you. And you don't want to go back and be looking at an empty chair.'

The tram was packed and Helen had to stand, swaying as it rattled round corners. She had gone to the station straight from school and her satchel dragged at her shoulders. Rain bladdered at the windows. She hoped Sandy wouldn't have a rough crossing.

When they got to Cyclamen Terrace, Helen thought Aunt Violet was looking rather too closely for dust, but she decided that was an uncharitable thought, considering

Aunt Violet had just waved her only son off to war. Maybe she couldn't help that peering, narrow-eyed look.

They sat in the parlour – Mrs Magee had left everything ready and Helen carefully wet the tea and carried everything in. Mama had baked scones.

'Quite nice,' pronounced Aunt Violet.

Granny admired Mama's new brooch. Aunt Violet said it was pretty but kept her hands clasped in her lap when Granny offered it to her. As if the shamrock would somehow contaminate her with its Irishness.

'Did you find *your* brooch, Aunt Violet?' Helen asked.

Aunt Violet looked puzzled, then said, 'Och! Yes. It was the strangest thing! I'd left it in my other jacket. I was sure I'd taken it off but when I went to get ready for the Ladies' Guild last night, there it was, still safely pinned to the lapel.'

They all rejoiced loudly, and Helen couldn't resist saying, 'It must have been that wee prayer I said to Saint Anthony.'

Aunt Violet looked at Mama. 'I hope this isn't the kind of thing you encourage, Eileen?'

'What sort of thing?'

'All that – well, mumbo-jumbo.'

'*Catholic* mumbo-jumbo, do you mean?'

Granny made an embarrassed noise in her throat and said it had turned out an awful evening and she hoped poor James would get a seat in the tram, and wasn't it time he was in. Everyone ignored her.

'It's only a wee thing we say,' Helen explained, wishing now that she hadn't taken the opportunity to tease

Aunt Violet. She should have known it wouldn't end well, and there was Mama looking tight and cross, with those red spots of anger burning in her pale cheeks.

'*We*? Helen – you've come to church with us since you were a baby,' Aunt Violet said. 'You know perfectly well it's nonsense to pray to *saints*.' She said it in the same contemptuous way Nora had said *British*. 'Nobody can intercede for you with God.'

'It was only a *joke*,' Helen muttered. 'I didn't pray about your brooch. I don't even …' A warning glance from Mama made her trail off. She glared into her teacup.

'Please don't tell my daughter that her mother's faith is nonsense,' Mama said in a calm voice that made Helen shiver.

'Violet,' Granny said, 'did you show Eileen and Helen the new photo of Sandy? We collected it today,' she said. 'There's a big one for the mantelpiece, but you have some snaps too, don't you?'

'Please could I have one?'

Helen loved the idea of having a snap of Sandy, keeping it in her purse … Or was that rather a Florence Bell thing to do? Better to frame it, perhaps, and set it on her bedside table.

Aunt Violet inclined her head graciously. 'If you promise to take *very* good care of it.'

She handed Helen a postcard-sized photo, and there was Sandy in shades of grey, staring seriously out at her.

He had, of course, sat for a portrait last year, when he'd joined up. But now he had been promoted to lieutenant, and had had a new uniform made – the old one had been damaged beyond repair when he was injured. Last year he had looked like a boy dressed up – the way all the boys at school looked when they paraded with the Cadet Corps on speech day; now he looked like, well, what he'd said on the train that night, 'a dashing young officer', with the stripe on his cuff to show he had been wounded. She must find a way, next time she went to Derryward, to let Nora know she had this precious picture.

'He's very like himself, isn't he?' Granny said.

'He's very handsome,' Mama said. 'Is he getting a look of his daddy, do you think?'

Aunt Violet seemed to appreciate Mama's attempts to be friendly. 'And is there any chance of your other nephew joining up?' she asked.

Which proved, Helen thought, that Sandy mustn't talk to his mother very much – otherwise he'd have told her about Michael.

Mama sighed and gave Helen a not-this-again look, but she smiled at Aunt Violet and said, 'I don't think his father can spare him from the farm.'

This was not the right thing to say.

'*I* can't spare my Sandy!' Aunt Violet said, her voice several tones higher than usual. 'And me a widow. But we all make sacrifices. At least, some of us do. Those of us who know our duty. I suppose loyalty doesn't mean the same down there.'

She said 'down there' as if Derryward were hell – but there were people in Belfast, Helen knew, people a few streets away, who thought exactly as Uncle Sean did.

'And of course, Sandy is very brave – well, he's been brought up to think of his country before himself. *Ulster*,' Aunt Violet added, as if there was any doubt about that.

Helen was about to say that Ulster wasn't a country; it was one of four provinces *of Ireland*, but she didn't feel brave enough for that conversation – not with Aunt Violet. Better to keep it personal.

So, stammering in her eagerness to defend Michael and, somehow, Mama, she said, 'But – but Michael *wants* to join up. *Lots* of Catholics have. He's determined! He and Uncle Sean have had all sorts of fights about it.'

'Helen,' said Mama in a warning voice. 'I'm sure Aunt Violet doesn't want to know all about my family.'

'Well, she should! Michael's *just* as brave as Sandy. Braver, maybe, because he's having to go against his own family! Sandy just went with everyone's blessing.' Oh no, now she sounded as if she was being disloyal to *Sandy*. She said a silent apology to the serious, greyish version of him in the photo she was still clutching. 'I mean –'

'Eileen,' Granny said, 'these scones are delicious. You must give me the recipe.'

'But it's *your* recipe,' Mama said, and they both managed tinkling laughs.

This might have helped the atmosphere had Aunt Violet not said, 'There's no comparison! Sandy has proved his courage in the battlefield. He has been mentioned in dispatches twice! He is a very fine young man.' Her breath huffed down her nose.

'I *know*,' Helen said. 'Sandy's the bravest person I know. I'm just saying Michael's a – a fine young man too.'

A hammering at the door silenced her. *Rattle-rattle-bang.* They all looked at each other.

Mama's brow crinkled. 'Could James have forgotten his latch-key?'

'It doesn't sound like Papa,' Helen said.

'And it couldn't be a telegram,' Granny said. 'Not banging like that.'

'Maybe it's children playing knock-and-run.'

'Oh, they never play that in our street,' Aunt Violet said.

'It's not the weather for children to be out playing anything,' Granny said.

Rattle-rattle-bang-BANG!

'Someone should go.'

Mama stood up and crossed the room to the window. She drew back the heavy brocade curtain and peered out into the dark. Helen saw her back tense.

'Who is it?' she said.

Mama shook her head. 'Nobody – I'll deal with it.' She went to the parlour door, saying, 'Stay where you are. It's nothing to worry about.'

Which was clearly a lie.

Afterwards, Helen wished she had obeyed Mama and stayed safely in the parlour.

8.

She rushed into the hall, leaving the door open behind her.

Michael stood in the porch. *Michael*? In *Belfast*? He wasn't wearing a cap, and he swayed as if the porch tiles were the floor of a hurtling tram.

'Helen, go back into the parlour,' Mama ordered. 'I'll deal with Michael.'

'I don't need to be *dealt with*,' Michael shouted.

He didn't sound like himself. He was loud and slurred. His cheeks were flushed, his coat torn; a bruise purpled his left eye.

He seemed to notice Helen for the first time and held out his arms to her.

'Helen!' he cried, as if he hadn't seen her for years. 'My wee cousin!' He buried his face in her shoulder.

Helen froze, her own arms stiff at her sides. Michael smelt like the doorway of McCann's public house which Aunt Violet always hurried her past, tutting, on the way to church on Sundays.

'I'm on my way to join up!' he shouted. 'I'm going to be a soldier. I'm going to fight for Ireland.'

And then she heard Aunt Violet's voice behind her.

'Eileen? What on earth …?'

Michael looked up at her. He was pale and wild, his hair messed up, rain running down his face.

'Who the hell are you?' he said.

But before Aunt Violet could answer – Helen thought she could actually hear her gasp – his face turned the colour of old cheese and he belched. Aunt Violet drew back, flapping her hands. Michael clasped his hand to his mouth, and tried to rush back outside, but it was too late – he vomited all over the tiled porch floor. And then slumped quietly down the wall, legs akimbo, boots sliding through the mess, looking nothing at all like a fine young man.

9.

If Papa hadn't come home just then, strong enough to deal with a semi-conscious drunk, it would have been much worse. *But even so,* Helen thought, sitting on her window-seat looking out at the rain shimmering in the street-lights, *it's bad enough.* Getting rid of Aunt Violet and Granny; dragging Michael into the house; cleaning up – and all the time Helen had hovered in doorways, scared of this unrecognisable person who was Michael and yet not Michael, but not quite able to take herself off to bed, which is what Mama kept telling her to do.

'You're neither use nor ornament, Helen,' she said.

Helen was officially in bed, but too restless for sleep. Wrapped in her camel-hair dressing gown which was getting too small, she hugged her knees. The house was silent round her. For ages there had been footsteps back and forth across the landing to the guest room, and muttering from Mama and Papa's room. She hadn't been able to make out many words – 'drunk' was one and 'poor Bridie' and 'some kind of fight' and 'a miracle he made it here' – but mainly just mutter-mutter, their voices rising and falling, mostly sounding worried.

She felt very alone, but also very conscious of Michael next door, even though there had been silence from that room for ages now. From the hallway the clock whirred and then chimed – *nine, ten, eleven.* Sandy's boat would still be on the Irish Sea. She hoped Aunt Violet wouldn't tell him. He had liked Michael, and now he would think …

She would have to get a frame for Sandy's photo.

Helen yawned. She would be tired tomorrow in school – and of course she couldn't tell Mabel why. Not even Florence Bell could have romanticised that disgusting scene in the porch. Michael had no *right* to be that shouting, drunken, *embarrassing* person – she wanted always to think of him carrying orphan lambs down from the lambing pens, offering her a birthday kitten, meeting her on the station platform, leaning against the trap, grinning.

I hate him, she thought.

She needed to go to the lavatory. Sighing, she pulled her dressing-gown belt tight, and, feeling her way in the dark, because she didn't want to risk putting on a light and perhaps worrying Mama and Papa if they weren't already asleep, she crept along the landing. On the way back, she couldn't help pausing outside the guest-room door. It was slightly ajar, but she could hear – nothing. Not even breathing. Was Michael all right? Could people *die* from being drunk? She shifted her weight, and the floorboard creaked.

'Hello?' A hoarse whisper, but definitely Michael. Alive.

'It's only me, Helen,' she whispered through the crack.

'Can you come in? Please?'

'I suppose so.'

She was still cross, but sort of proud too, to be wanted. She tiptoed in. The guest room was tiny, and very dark. She banged her hip on a chair and stifled an *ouch*.

'Put on the light, silly,' Michael whispered.

He was hardly in a position to call *her* silly, but she switched on the electric light, a little afraid of what it would reveal. Michael blinked at the sudden glare – at Derryward they had oil lamps. He was in bed, wearing an old pyjama jacket of Papa's, his blackened eye half-closed inside a vivid purple bruise.

She held back, twisting her dressing gown chord.

'What happened your eye?' She was an icicle, still hating him.

Michael shook his head, and winced. 'I got lost. I remembered the name of your street but – I got the wrong tram. Ended up – God, I don't know where, but it was rough.'

'So – you got in a *fight*?'

'Bit of a scuffle, aye. Some fellas ...'

'And you went *drinking* with them?'

'No. That was afterwards. Thought I'd have one to calm my nerves.'

'Hardly *one*?'

I sound, she thought, *like Aunt Violet.*

He grimaced. 'I don't even remember getting here – it's all a bit – did I disgrace myself?'

'You disgraced all of us.' She told him what had happened.

Michael's face stiffened in horror, and went even paler. The ice inside Helen started to melt. A Derryward memory twitched at her, one she didn't often allow herself to think of. She had been about eight, and had found a lamb dead in the field, ravaged by a dog or a fox; its entrails spilled on the grass. She had sickened instantly, running back to the yard with vomit on her dress, wailing, and Nora had laughed at the state of her.

But Michael had taken her to the pump and cleaned her up, and told her that these things happened on farms. He'd led her up and down the lane on the chestnut mare, until she almost forgot the lamb.

She sat on the bed, forcing herself not to gag at the lingering smell of alcohol.

'It's all right,' she said. 'You'll probably never have to see Aunt Violet and Granny again.' After all, they were her family, not his.

'But Aunt Eileen and Uncle James ...' He rubbed one hand over his face.

She patted his other hand. 'Don't worry,' she said. 'I'll try to do something bad in school tomorrow – take the attention off you. I didn't get my prep done so Peg Leg Perry will probably have conniptions.'

He gave a weak smile. 'I'll be gone by then,' he said. 'Joined up.'

'I don't think the army will like that black eye.' *Or*, she thought, *the stink of alcohol.*

'They can't afford to be fussy these days.'

'Even so, you don't just sign up and march away. You'll have time to go back and see Aunt Bridie and Uncle Sean.'

'*No.*'

'But Aunt Bridie will be so worried! Mama said her heart was broken!'

Michael looked away, his lips tightening. 'I won't go back. *Ever.*' He sighed and touched his sore eye. 'I didn't get this in a street brawl. This was my da. He told me I was no son of his. If I join the British army I'm dead to him.'

And to Helen's shock, his dark eyes filled with tears.

'Don't!' She pulled her hand away from his. He must still be inebriated. Boys – young men – well, they didn't *cry*. He was supposed to be going to war; he couldn't go round acting like Florence Bell.

Michael blinked away the tears. 'I'm sorry,' he said. 'I thought I was doing the right thing. I really do believe every Irishman should join up and fight. But I could hardly stand up to my da – how'm I going to stand up to the Hun – the Germans?'

Helen had no answer to this, except a pathetic, 'Of course you will.' There was an uneasy silence, which she broke by saying, 'It's late, and you're' – she was about to say 'drunk', but changed it to 'tired. And I have school tomorrow. Let's not talk about this now.'

The funny thing was, though, she thought, settling down in her now cold sheets, kicking them to try to warm them up, that Michael was more like her than she realised – not really knowing which side he was on.

10.

A cavalcade of navy coats streamed down the school driveway to the big iron gates in School Gardens. Florence Bell walked in front of Helen, her long fair curls spilling over her shoulders, arm in arm with a smaller girl.

'Who's she with?' Helen asked. Belfast Collegiate girls didn't go in for walking arm in arm; they left that kind of soppiness to the girls' schools.

'Jessie McGrath. Remember her father was killed just before Christmas? She must be Florence's new best friend.'

'Until Miss Linden comes back,' Helen said. 'Then she'll be in her element, carrying her books and sucking up.'

Mabel giggled, then looked stricken. 'Are we horrible?'

'We're not laughing at people being *dead*. We're making fun of Florence being so – well, so …'

They were trying to think of the exact word to describe Florence when Mabel said, 'Helen? Who's that soldier waving at you?'

For one ridiculous moment, Helen thought, *Sandy! He must be home again*, even though she had had a letter yesterday – a proper letter, just for her, saying that his course was going well but that he couldn't wait to join his men again next week.

But the young private waving from the school gates, looking self-conscious in new khaki, nowhere near as smart as Sandy's tailored officer's uniform, was Michael.

Helen waved back. 'It's Michael,' she said.

'I wish *I'd* a handsome soldier waiting for me at the school gates,' Mabel said.

'Don't be silly; he's my cousin,' Helen said, though she glowed at hearing Michael described as handsome.

His black eye had faded, and with it had faded Helen's memories of the scene in the porch. He had been with them for a few days now, quiet and embarrassed at first, too restless for the narrow house. He had had chats with Papa, and gone to mass with Mama on Sunday, and she had come home with a kind of glow Helen wasn't used to.

'It was lovely not being on my own for once,' she had said when Helen commented on it. And she had smiled up at Michael in a way that made him blush and fidget. Helen had said nothing. Mama worshipping alone was one of the things they didn't mention. Years ago Helen, dazzled by the white perfection of Nora's First Holy Communion dress, and somehow hoping she might get one too, had begged if she could go to Mama's church – from the little she could glean, it seemed so romantic, with its candles and Latin and the possibility of a white dress. Papa, in a grim, un-Papa-like voice, had said she mustn't ask again, and she understood dimly that there was something very forbidden about mass.

Michael had refused to go back to Derryward to say goodbye, and he wouldn't even write.

'Write!' he'd said when Mama had suggested it. He gave a bitter laugh. 'Da told me exactly what he'd do with any letter from me – straight into the fire!'

'Och, Michael, he couldn't mean that.' But Helen remembered the black eye, and wasn't so sure.

'He meant it all right.' And Michael hadn't said another word for the whole evening.

But he looked happy and carefree now in the darkening winter afternoon, starting up the driveway to meet them, affecting nonchalance in the new uniform, but clearly loving the effect he was creating, mostly on the older girls.

'I hope Miss Thomas doesn't see him,' Mabel warned Helen. 'She's probably lurking somewhere.'

But luck was on their side – perhaps Miss Thomas had had a tip-off about the sixth-form girls who were rumoured to have been powdering their noses at the back gate – and they reached Michael without being intercepted.

Michael grabbed Helen's satchel from her and slung it over his shoulder, where it looked incongruous against the khaki.

'I'm leaving tomorrow,' he said. 'Down south for training. So Aunt Eileen says I can take you to – Caprini's is it? – for an ice to celebrate.' He nodded at Mabel. 'You too, if you want.'

Mabel wrinkled her brow. 'I'd love to, but Mother'll worry if I don't turn up at home.'

'Florence can take a message,' Helen suggested. 'Hey, Florrie?'

Florence had been too busy foisting her secrets onto Jessie to notice Michael, but now she turned and stared slack-mouthed, walking backwards a few steps, trailing Jessie with her.

'Will you run in and tell my mother I'll be late back?' Mabel asked.

'Jessie's coming to tea with me,' Florence said importantly.

'So? You'll still have to walk past my house. Oh go on, Florrie. I'll do the same for you.'

'If *you* ever get asked out to Caprini's by a soldier,' Helen couldn't resist adding.

'So – I should tell your mother you've gone to Caprini's with a Tommy?' Florence said, her large eyes bulging.

That's her way of telling us she's noticed that he's only a private, Helen thought. Most of the old Collegians were officers. Jessie stood on one leg and looked like she would love to be going anywhere, with anyone, rather than to tea with Florence.

'You do – I suppose you *know* him?' Florence asked.

Mabel looked at Michael and then at Helen, her eyes sparkling.

'Oh no,' Helen said. 'We just picked him up in the street. We always try to find a stray Tommy to take us out on a Thursday.'

'If we can't find a sailor,' Mabel added.

'We'll probably go on to a music hall,' Michael said, with a grin.

Florence gaped.

Helen linked arms with both Michael and Mabel, and they set off down School Gardens to the main road, giggling. Michael walked so fast – as if he were marching already – that the girls had to make little skips to keep up, which made Mabel giggle even more.

It felt festive, though it shouldn't. This wasn't 1914, with the war just begun and everyone predicting a swift and glorious victory. Helen remembered Dr Allen's speech in prayers about the young generation being 'privileged to be asked to prove itself in the theatre of war'. As a second-former, she had been very impressed. People knew better now: even she, a schoolgirl, had seen name upon name of the dead in school magazines and on the Roll of Honour in the school chapel. She remembered Sandy, on that long, tiring train journey, saying he couldn't tell his mother what it was really like. Had he told Michael? She remembered them in the farmyard, hammering the palings together. They had looked like men, in their own world, smoking and chatting. She had been jealous. And if he had told Michael what it was really like – well, it hadn't put Michael off.

She tightened her arm in her cousin's. *He'll be gone tomorrow*, she thought. *And Sandy will be back in the front line soon.*

She wasn't jealous now.

FEBRUARY 1916

11.

It was a dank February afternoon. The days were lengthening but even so, it felt to Helen, letting herself into the house and shaking the rain off her school hat, as if spring would never come. Mama's voice called from the parlour before she had even hung up her coat. She sighed – she'd been hoping to sneak up to her bedroom and start the new Elsie Oxenham book Mabel had lent her.

Mama was on the *chaise longue*, a rug over her legs. Her hair was not as neatly done as usual. Perhaps she had fallen asleep and ruffled it. She had a khaki muffler on her lap but it was only a few rows long, slipping off its needles. The lamps hadn't been lit and the fire was almost out and, though the room was clean, it looked somehow forsaken.

'I've been waiting for you to build up the fire,' Mama said. 'You know coal dust makes me cough.'

'Sorry, Mama.'

Helen bent down in front of the grate and gave the fire a good riddling. There was a full scuttle of coal on the hearth and a basket of logs. Surely Mama could have put on a couple of logs? She seemed to have shaken off the worst of the chestiness that plagued her every winter; she just seemed cross most of the time.

'There.' Helen stood back as the fire, sullenly at first, and then with more conviction, leapt into life.

She frowned at her reflection in the over-mantel mirror, and pushed some wisps of hair behind her ears. A single plait was harder to keep tidy. An envelope poked out from behind one of the Staffordshire dogs. She pulled it out, and another one came with it, both Forces envelopes, both addressed to her. One was in Sandy's familiar script; the other in Michael's writing. This was the second time he had written from the training camp. 'You know I can't write home,' he'd said on the morning they had gone to see him off. 'So I'll write to you instead.'

Sandy had written only a few days ago: she hadn't expected a letter so soon, especially as he had hinted that they were moving up the line for what he called 'some action'. Two in one day! All thoughts of *Rosaly's New School* fled, even though Mabel had said it was first-rate. She couldn't wait to get up to her bedroom.

But Mama said, 'Don't bother with those now, Helen. I've been on my own all day. Why are you so late?'

'Miss Cassidy asked me to stay behind.' She slid the letters into her blazer pocket. 'She wants me to join her special class after school.'

'Special class? You mean you need extra help? Your father won't like –'

'No!' Helen flopped down in one of the armchairs. 'The opposite, really. It's her scholarship class – for girls she thinks are promising. It's mostly older girls – Edith Hamilton and Patricia McBride – she's never asked *anyone* from the fourth before!'

Her voice squeaked with excitement, even though she wasn't really sure she wanted to join the class. That would be something to tell Sandy when she wrote back! If she was ever allowed to read his letter.

'And what's the point of it?'

Helen forced herself not to sigh. 'The *point* is to help us prepare for college.'

'*College*? Why would you want that? Don't tell me you want to be a teacher like your father?'

'I – I don't know. But maybe.'

'No,' Mama said. 'You're only fourteen. I don't want your head filled with nonsense about college.'

'*Papa* will want me to go.'

Papa was always telling Helen to make the most of her opportunities at Belfast Collegiate. He hated seeing the children in his own school going to the mill or the rope-works or the shipyard at fourteen, even the bright ones.

There was a heavy silence before Mama said, 'Papa will want you to come home after school and make yourself useful. You've no idea how long the days are for me here, alone.'

Helen chewed the insides of her cheeks.

'And what's the point in teaching? You'd only do it for a few years until you married. Unless you *want* to be an old maid like your precious Miss Cassidy?' She twirled her heavy gold wedding ring on her thin finger.

'I may not have a choice,' Helen said. 'All the boys are getting killed in France.'

In her pocket, the envelopes rustled. She hoped they weren't being crumpled.

'Don't be dramatic, Helen. And talking of France – what did you do with those letters you lifted from the mantelpiece?'

'They're addressed to me.'

'You're too young to be writing to soldiers.'

'Mama! Michael and Sandy are *family*.'

'I might as well have lost my family when I married into your father's.' Helen hated it when Mama said things like that. 'Goodness knows if we'll ever be invited back home again.' Mama sometimes called Derryward 'home'.

'Don't say that! Will we not go for Easter as usual?'

Mama shook her head. 'I don't know. Sean and Bridie blame *us* for Michael joining up.'

'Why?'

'We sheltered him. Your father helped him find out where he needed to go. And *Sandy* – goodness knows what nonsense *he* put into Michael's head. I don't know why you had to take Sandy to Derryward that day. It's caused nothing but bother.'

The unfairness of this stung like a dart. 'But Michael was planning to join up for ages! It was nothing to do with Sandy!'

'Well, that's not what Sean and Bridie think. Now, will you go and make some tea?'

Helen wanted very much to tell her mother to get her own tea, but she made herself put on the trying-too-hard voice she'd been using a great deal recently to say, 'Will I bring in some muffins, and we could toast them? There's some of that damson jelly Granny brought round yesterday.'

She couldn't escape with the precious letters until Papa came in, and then, with a leap of relief, she said she had lots of prep and dashed up to her bedroom. She closed the door and scrambled on to the bed, not bothering to take off her shoes.

She pulled the two envelopes out of her pocket and smoothed them. Which should she open first? It *mattered*. If she opened Sandy's first was that saying she liked him better than Michael? Or *vice versa*?

Then again, she had had a letter from Sandy most recently, which made it Michael's turn. She took a paper-knife from the desk by her bed, and slid open the top of Michael's envelope.

It was short. He was enjoying camp life. The other lads were good sport. There was a lot of drill and trench-digging and bayonet practice. The sergeant was a demon, the food not as good as at home. They were all impatient to get to France and do some proper fighting. The fields of Kildare were lush and green and full of beautiful horses, but he missed the rough hills around Derryward. That was quite poetic, for Michael. She grinned, and placed the letter in the handkerchief box where she kept her special things.

All Sandy's letters were there. He wrote every week or so, and at first, remembering their conversation in the train, she had been nervous that his letters would be full of unwelcome horrors – and annoyed with herself, for hadn't she begged him to be honest? – but the most gruesome detail so far had only been about a rat. His platoon were a good lot, mostly Belfast lads like himself, though mainly inexperienced. One of them, who Sandy would only call Private C, was a bit windy – it took Helen a while to realise that meant *cowardly* – and needed a good bit of jollying along. *Like Mama*, Helen thought guiltily. But his second lieutenant, Robbie McGivern – now he was a great lad; the sort of lad he'd been on rugby teams with; they were old pals already. 'You get to know a man pretty quickly out here,' he had written.

She pulled a single sheet out of the envelope. It wasn't as neat as usual, the handwriting sloping downwards on the page, the words smudged in places.

She knew before she read a single word, that it was going to be the horrible truth she had begged for and dreaded.

12.

My dear Helen,

We've had a sticky time since I last wrote. Won't bore you with details. But we've lost some good men, and are at the wound-licking stage. I AM A1, YOU MUSTN'T WORRY ABOUT ME, NOT A SCRATCH.

Then the writing started to grow bigger and messier. Sometimes he was digging in so hard that the paper was nearly torn. It looked almost as though he were – well, not quite sober.

I think I told you about young C? Never took to army life. Even miles back from the line, he was slack and windy. I told you there was a big push coming? Usual thing; waiting all night to attack at dawn. And C's whimpering and saying he's sick – and that's bad for the other lads. Panic in a trench – last thing you need. He'd got the wind up everybody. I told him to report sick – it was all I could think of, I just wanted him out of there.

Anyway the MO sent him back with a flea in his ear and told him to be a man. Or so I hear. Because he never came back. And in all the confusion – we attacked next morning – I think we thought he was dead anyway. And I don't mind telling you, I thought, well good riddance to him. We'd lost Robbie in the attack – in the worst way, hit in the stomach, died in agony. I didn't see it – but I heard it from the sergeant afterwards. And I couldn't stop thinking about that.

Helen gulped. She had a horrible image of Robbie – in her imagination he looked just like Sandy – with his guts spilling everywhere. Like that long-ago lamb at Derryward, bleeding into the grass. She swallowed and forced herself to read on. At times she had to peer and squint to decipher the writing.

But late that day C was found and arrested for desertion. He was court-martialled. They asked me to report on his character because I knew him better than the Captain, who'd only arrived. I said he wasn't a brave soldier and his influence on the other men was poor. So they passed the extreme sentence.

Do you know what that is, Helen? He was shot. By men of his own platoon. And maybe I could have stopped it. Maybe I could have pleaded for him. But I didn't. I was angry with him. I wanted him to die. Because Robbie was dead and that little piece of NOTHING was alive. And didn't deserve to be.

It happened this morning. I didn't shoot him myself, but I had to give the order. The men are all upset. I –

The letter tailed off there. Helen turned the page but

all that was written on the back – more neatly now – was

> *Sorry, you don't want to know all this. To be honest*
> *I've had more than a tot of rum tonight. Filthy stuff.*
> *Don't worry. Like I said I am A1. DON'T TELL*
> *ANYONE.*
> *And write back if you can spare the time.*
> *Sandy*

★ ★ ★

Helen played with her dinner, but couldn't force herself to swallow anything.

'I hope you aren't sickening for anything?' Mama asked.

Don't worry, Helen thought, *I know you're the only person allowed to be ill in this house.*

'I ate too many muffins at tea,' she said. 'Could I be excused? I have a letter to write.'

But she sat on her bed with her writing pad until her hands cramped with cold, and couldn't find any words at all.

MARCH 1916

13.

By half-term – late this year as Easter wasn't until near the end of April – the lower fourth had given up hope of Miss Linden ever returning. Annoyingly, it was Florence Bell, swollen with news and importance, who confirmed it.

'Mummy met her in Robinson and Cleaver's buying pillowcases. She's staying home to comfort her poor parents.' Florence sighed with the deliciousness of it. 'They are *stricken* with grief.'

'So you'll need to find a new mistress to moon over,' Helen said, rummaging in her desk for her algebra. 'What about Miss Thomas?'

Even Florence giggled. 'Those whiskers!'

'Miss Cassidy's the nicest,' Helen said. She didn't go in for pashes – certainly not on *teachers* – but she liked how Miss Cassidy kept on treating her the same even though she had refused to join the scholarship class. Helen couldn't imagine Miss Cassidy leaving her job to comfort her parents. Yet everyone seemed to think Miss Linden was doing exactly the right thing. Was she? If Michael – if anything *happened* – would Nora give up her dreams to comfort Aunt Bridie? But then Nora's dreams probably involved staying at home anyway, until she married. And Helen *mustn't* think thoughts like that about Michael, who was still training and in no personal danger whatsoever.

Unlike Sandy. But she couldn't let her thoughts stray in that direction.

'We might get a new history teacher,' she said. 'We've learned *nothing* with Peg Leg.'

The classroom door swung open, and one of the older girls stood in the doorway: Edith Hamilton, a quiet, clever girl Helen had always liked.

'I have an announcement about the school mag,' Edith said, her clear voice making even the boys shut up and listen. 'As you know, Miss Linden was the editor, and so nothing much has been done lately. Miss Cassidy's taken over now, but if we're going to have a mag this term we need volunteers. To write articles, edit, that sort of thing. You need to be able to spell. The meeting's at break.'

When she had gone, Helen looked at Mabel. 'We can spell,' she said.

Mabel wrinkled her nose. 'It's spring. I'd much rather be outside with a hockey ball than editing reports of rugby and death. That's all it is these days. Too depressing.'

'Not *all*.'

But Mabel had a point. The magazine was called *The Collegian*, a slim, buff-covered volume which appeared every term. Some of it was dull – Dr Allen's prize day speeches and accounts of life in India or Africa from some old boy who'd been there for decades. (There never seemed to be articles from old girls.) There were rugby and hockey and cricket reports, depending on the season, and lists of exam successes and prizes.

And then, since the autumn magazine of 1914, war news. Enthusiastic at first – details of old boys who'd joined up, and some old girls who'd gone to be nurses.

Breezy letters home from the Front, full of affection for the old school. An account of the setting up of the Old Boys' Parcel Fund, and the concerts held to raise money. The whole school went war-crazy for a time – girls were even allowed to knit at recreation.

In December 1914, the magazine reported the school's first casualty. Helen hadn't known Owen McArthur – he had left in 1908 and had been a regular soldier before the war. But like everyone else, she had felt a mixture of sadness and a kind of guilty thrill on reading about his death. After that, the casualties came too steadily for individual obituaries. In the last magazine, winter 1915, there had been five, two of them boys Helen remembered, class- and team-mates of Sandy's. She always sent the magazine out to Sandy, even though she thought it must depress him these days. There was a Roll of Honour, amended every edition, of all the boys serving. It was always out of date by the time it was printed.

'Sorry,' Mabel said. 'Not my kind of thing. And anyway, Winifred's organising extra hockey practice for third-eleven hopefuls.'

Last term, Helen would never have signed up without Mabel. But, feeling shy, she went at break to the sixth-form room where the meeting was held. Unlike the Old Boys' Parcels Committee, which was mostly girls, there was a good mixture of boys and girls, including George Rae, the only other person from the fourth. He made room for her at a double desk.

'Should have guessed you'd be here,' he said. 'You always beat me at composition.'

'Well, you always beat me at Latin,' Helen said, but she couldn't help glowing.

It was true she was good at writing. *Perhaps*, she thought, with a burst of ambition, *I'll be a lady journalist.* She wasn't sure there was such a thing, but she could ask Miss Cassidy.

As it turned out, only the sixth-formers would be allowed to write articles. Miss Cassidy, glancing down at her clipboard and then round the room, said, 'Now, I need a team of really methodical people to check the Roll of Honour – it's such an important job. Edith? Would you take that on? With – let's see – Helen and George?'

Helen bit her lip with pleasure. She guessed that the Roll of Honour would involve painstaking work, transcribing details of the old boys' regiments, rank and such information as their families had sent back to the school, sometimes through younger brothers and sisters. And yes, it might be depressing, as Mabel thought, because very often amending the list meant adding in the fact that someone had been killed or injured, but even so, it felt important to be trusted with something like that rather than just the hockey teams or the debating society reports.

'It's sort of war work,' she explained to Mama that evening. She had deliberately waited until Papa was home, because she knew Papa would want her to do it. He had been a pupil at Belfast Collegiate himself. 'I know you didn't want me to stay for Miss Cassidy's class but this is different.'

'You'll have to get the tram home alone,' Mama pointed out.

'I don't mind. I sometimes do anyway, if Mabel has hockey practice.'

Papa smiled. 'I'd love to think of you helping with the school magazine,' he said. 'I had a few articles in it myself about a hundred years ago.'

Mama sighed. 'I suppose it's all right,' she said. 'James, would you put more coal on that fire? There's no heat off it at all.'

***

Next day, Helen turned up hot and breathless after hockey, to find Edith and George already sitting round a desk, sorting out letters and scraps of newsprint from a fat manila folder.

'Sorry,' she said, pulling over a third chair. She didn't want Edith to think she was unreliable. 'Miss Thomas erupted into the changing rooms to check everyone's tunic wasn't too short.'

Edith looked amused. 'She did that to us yesterday. She must be having one of her clamp-downs on legs.' She grinned at George, who was blushing. 'You boys don't know how lucky you are.'

Helen's job was to sift through a pile of letters and cuttings and add anything relevant to the Roll of Honour.

'Just write it in as neatly as you can,' Edith said. 'Oh – and put a line through anything that's out of date.

The secretary will type up a new list when you're finished. You can do R-Z.'

'That means I get Sandy!' Helen said, and Edith smiled. 'That's why I kept it for you.'

'Do you have anyone at the Front?' Helen asked George, who was copying out the details from a casualty report, his face even more serious than usual.

He shook his head. 'We're Quakers,' he said. 'So we're pacifists.'

Helen wondered if that made things easier or harder, but didn't feel she knew him well enough to ask, even though they'd been in class together for years. Boys and girls didn't mix very much out of lessons. If the war were still on when George was old enough – would being a conscientious objector be easier or harder than fighting?

'We have a friend – from our meeting – who's out there as a stretcher bearer,' George went on, as if he could tell that Helen was interested. 'He wanted to help but not to engage in combat.'

'I think you'd need to be very brave to do that,' Edith said. 'Hugh and Gilbert have told me something about it.'

Helen had forgotten that she had two brothers in the army.

'Yes. But some of his family think even doing that is supporting armed conflict,' George said. 'They wouldn't even read his letters.'

Gosh, thought Helen, *that doesn't sound very pacifist.* She went to say something but George pushed his glasses up his nose and nodded at his papers. 'Better get on with this.'

Helen took the hint and sifted through her pile of cuttings. She made herself go in strict alphabetical order, but even so Sandy – *Alexander Charles Reid, Second Lieutenant, Royal Irish Rifles (BCS, 1907-1914)* – was one of the first names she had to deal with. Taking a ruler from her satchel she drew a careful line through 'Second' to show that he had been promoted, and then through the sentence *After being seriously wounded in September, Second Lieutenant Reid is making a good recovery in hospital in England.* She wasn't expected, of course, to write the amended bit herself – there was a small white piece of paper, the standard form the school sent home requesting information, and in Aunt Violet's spiky copperplate was written: 'Lieutenant Reid has returned to his regiment and is fighting the good fight in France.'

It wasn't exactly how Helen would have expressed it, but it wasn't *untrue* – it was just too simple, too naïve. Sandy's recent letters hadn't been as upsetting as the one about Robbie and C, but they certainly never mentioned 'fighting the good fight'. She had eventually replied to that shocking letter, but had found nothing better to say than, 'That sounds horrid. Poor you.' Which she knew wasn't what he had hoped for.

He had apologised: 'I don't think I was in my right mind when I burdened you with all that. Too much of the old rum ration. Just as well officers are trusted to censor their own letters! Sometimes I forget you're only fourteen. Please put it out of your head.' Helen had been relieved, but also felt as if she had failed him.

The next three names had no changes except that Arthur Sheldon had been promoted. She vaguely remembered Arthur as a glittering head boy. It was easy to see him as a captain. But then there were two in a row – Henry Taylor and Cyril Vance – about whose deaths, one in action, one from wounds, she had to copy the details, and when she had finished, taking particular care in inking a neat black cross by each name, she felt quite miserable.

She remembered packing an old boys' parcel for Cyril Vance, saying to Mabel, 'Isn't Cyril Vance a horrid name?' She wished now she hadn't said that. She wondered if she would be given the same task next term, and what changes there would be. By the winter, many of the summer's leavers would have joined up and added their names to the list. She wondered if in Michael's school in the town near Derryward someone was doing something similar now: 'Michael O'Hare is training with the Royal Irish Regiment.' Or did the Christian Brothers who had taught him feel the same as Uncle Sean? Was his old school proud, or ashamed, like his family?

She remembered what George had said about his stretcher-bearer friend and his family not reading his letters. At least he had written. If only Michael would! Looking at these lists, name upon name of young men facing death every day, Helen wished he would change his mind. Letters were something to keep. She couldn't bear to think of anything happening to Sandy, but if it did, she knew she would be glad to have his letters.

And before long Michael, like Sandy, wouldn't be safe in camp. He'd be at the Front.

She touched Sandy's name, stroking the three words carefully with her finger as if by doing so she could protect him. Though there was nothing she could do to stop his name, by next term, or even next week, acquiring that neat black ink cross.

14.

A week later, in prayers, Dr Allen announced the death of another old boy. It was Edith's brother Hugh.

Helen only vaguely remembered Hugh – it was Gilbert, the younger brother, who had been on the rugby team with Sandy, but even so, it felt like the nearest death yet. All day Dr Allen's voice followed her around: 'He was operated on to amputate both legs, but he died of haemorrhage. Let us all remember him and his family in prayer.'

She and George went to the sixth-form room to finish off their work on the Roll of Honour. They divided Edith's cuttings between them without being asked, and neither quite liked to put the black cross against *Hugh Ross Hamilton, Lieutenant, Royal Irish Rifles (BCS, 1906-13)*. In the end, George did it, and they finished their task in silence, taking the amended lists to Miss Cassidy when they were done.

'Good work,' she said. She gave Helen a quick smile. 'No chance of you changing your mind about the scholarship class?'

Helen shook her head. 'Sorry, Miss Cassidy. My mother needs me.'

'Ah well, you've plenty of time yet. Sometimes I forget you're only fourteen.'

How funny, Helen thought, *that she should have said just the same as Sandy.*

'Is it not unfair for girls to have special coaching and not boys?' George asked as they walked together down the drive, Helen feeling self-conscious at walking with a boy she wasn't related to.

'I don't think so,' Helen said. 'It's *much* harder for girls to get to college than it is for boys.'

'Both my sisters are at Queen's,' George said. 'And *my* family was delighted for them. But then we're Quakers – that's how we think. Men and women should be treated equally.'

'I didn't know that,' Helen admitted. 'I wouldn't mind being a Quaker; I like the sound of that.'

George shrugged. 'You just are what you are. Like you're a Protestant.'

'I'm not really, though,' Helen said. 'I mean, not a proper one. I go to the Presbyterian church with my father and his family. But my mother's a Catholic.'

She didn't tend to talk about this in school. Belfast Collegiate was officially non-denominational but there weren't any Catholics there, because they had their own schools.

'A mixed marriage?' George said as if it were something interesting instead of, as Helen had always thought, a bit embarrassing. 'How did they meet?'

They had reached the school gates now, and as both seemed to want to keep talking, they leaned against the railings in a way that would have scandalised Miss Thomas.

This was a story Helen knew well. 'Mama came up from the country to look after a sick aunt. Papa was lodging in the house next door and he used to see her taking the aunt to the park in a wheel chair. She was very beautiful and he fell in love with her.' She imagined her long-ago mother, the sun on her brown hair, pushing the old lady in the chair, and Papa with the funny old-fashioned moustache that looked so odd in their wedding photo. 'Both their families were horrified. But she was over twenty-one so they had to make the best of it.'

'Sounds like *Romeo and Juliet*.'

'Hardly,' Helen said. 'Juliet was thirteen. Younger than me. And they *died*.' And then she blushed, at having in a way compared herself to Juliet in front of a boy. She played with the strap of her satchel. 'I should go and get the tram,' she said.

'I'll walk you to the tram stop,' George said.

They fell into step along the road, their black school shoes clomping along. Helen posted a letter to Michael at the pillar-box at the end of School Gardens. It was an important one because in it she suggested to Michael that he should write to his family. She knew he would object and remind her that his father had threatened to throw any such letter into the fire, but Helen had thought of a brilliant way round this: 'Send it to me,' she written, 'and I'll make sure it gets safely to your mother.'

She felt solemn dropping the letter into the pillar-box, and George gave her a quick glance, as if he was about to ask her about it, but he didn't.

On the corner of the main road, a newspaper boy, with sticky-up hair and sticky-out ears, shouted, 'Tele!' and thrust a Belfast Telegraph at them. Helen flinched from the headline – MORE ULSTER CASUALTIES. She wondered if George might buy a paper – it seemed the kind of odd, elderly thing he might do – but he brushed the boy off and went back to the subject of Helen's parents.

'So – why do you go to your father's church?' George asked. 'I thought children were normally brought up in their mother's religion?'

Helen was vague. This wasn't much spoken about in 22 Cyclamen Terrace.

'I think Papa's family just took over. Mama was ill when I was born. She's not very strong. By the time she was able to look after me, they'd had me baptised and everything. My grandfather said it would break his heart if his only granddaughter were brought up in the Catholic church. He said I'd be born into darkness.' She always imagined those words in capitals, haloed in infernal flames.

George shook his head.

'And Mama just gave in. I don't suppose she had much choice. But if I'd been brought up Catholic my life would have been completely different, wouldn't it?' She thought of her jealousy over Nora's First Communion dress. 'I'd have gone to a different school, *believed* something different.' She wasn't exactly sure *what* she would have believed except that it was something to do with praying to the Virgin Mary and the saints, and believing the priest *actually* changed the bread and wine into Christ's body and blood, which always sounded improbable. But exciting too; sort of romantic. 'Played different sports; maybe even learned *Irish* …' Though she wasn't sure if that was something you learned at school.

Even saying all these things out loud felt defiant: she could imagine Aunt Violet's lips disappearing inside her mouth. *I wonder,* she thought, *if I'd actually have ended up a different* person. She imagined herself at a convent school, the corridors filled with black-robed nuns, but she couldn't see her own face.

'Actually, lots of Presbyterians helped revive the Irish language, at least in Belfast,' George said. '*And* wanted an independent Ireland. Haven't you heard of the United Irishmen? The 1798 rebellion?'

Helen wrinkled her nose. 'Are you sure?'

'Quite sure. Don't you know *any* history? Apart from what we do with Perry, which is all British and Empire history anyway.'

Helen was silent, readjusting to this strange information. Surely it couldn't be right? She longed for the tram to come round the corner: talking to George was – *interesting,* but rather disturbing. Challenging, like Miss Cassidy telling her she must think things out for herself.

'I can lend you some books if you like,' George said. 'My father's a professor of Irish history. Things aren't as simple as you might think.'

'No,' she said. 'I mean – yes to the books.' (Though she wasn't sure she wanted to read the kind of books a professor might lend her.) And here, at last, was the tram, its shabby red and cream shining through the grey afternoon drizzle. 'And no, things *don't* feel simple to me. I just thought they were for everyone else.'

'No,' said George after a short pause. 'Not for everyone.'

APRIL 1916

AVRIL 1916

15.

Dear Helen,

I've thought about that suggestion about writing home. It's worth a try. I suppose we've all calmed down a bit since the day I walked out. And I'll be going into action soon; they don't keep you hanging around the way they used to – can't afford to. And it would mean a lot to think they've forgiven me. NOT THAT I THINK THEY HAVE.

So I've written a letter and here it is. DON'T POST IT. Give it to Nora as she will know the best time to give it to Mammy. DON'T EVEN MENTION IT TO DA. I've asked them to write back if they forgive me – if they still think of me as their son; and if not just to ignore the letter. I'd rather have silence than another row, even on the page.

Helen, it is a great comfort to know I can trust you. I always said you were the brainy one of the family.

Your loving cousin
Michael

Helen read the letter with mixed emotions. Pride that he trusted her with something so important. Worry that she wouldn't be able to deliver it. Because they hadn't been to Derryward for *ages*.

If only she could have gone alone one Saturday – but the very idea was ridiculous. She would never be allowed. She could explain to Papa and ask him to take her, but running to her father, asking a grown-up to sort it all out – wasn't that a very 'wee Helen' thing to do? Michael had asked her because he trusted her, because she wasn't 'wee Helen' any more. She would just have to pray that they would go to Derryward at Easter, and perhaps in the meantime she shouldn't mention the letter to Michael. He would assume that she had delivered it, and could start looking forward to a reply. That would be best.

16.

It was all right! They were all going to Derryward for Easter – even Papa. She could deliver the letter.

When Helen remembered what Mama had said about the O'Hares blaming Papa for helping Michael to enlist, she was a little worried. But she didn't want to say that in front of Mabel. They were in Caprini's as a treat on their way home from school. You weren't allowed to eat in school uniform, so they felt daredevil and end-of-termish. And anyway, as Mabel said, an ice-cream sundae in a cut-glass dish in a respectable café wasn't in quite the same league as the fish and chips in newspaper three prefects had been caught scoffing on the Lisburn Road last week.

'Lucky you,' Mabel said. 'Easter on a farm must be lovely – will there be lambs?' She sucked the tip of her ice-cream spoon.

'It's nice of you to pretend to be jealous,' Helen said, 'but you'll have a much better time in Dublin with your aunt. Having tea at the Shelbourne! Spending your birthday money in Switzer's!' These were only glamorous names to Helen; she had never been to Dublin, but she loved saying them as if they meant something to her.

'But it won't be half as much fun without you,' Mabel said mournfully. 'I can't think *why* your father said no. Aunt Jean's very respectable. She lives in Clontarf, near the beach.'

'I know.' Helen sighed.

She would have loved to go to Dublin with Mabel, and it wasn't true that Papa had refused the invitation: she simply hadn't asked him, because of the importance of getting the letter to Derryward. She still felt that she had somehow failed Sandy over his letter. She wasn't going to fail Michael. She felt quite noble and self-sacrificing.

'Derryward won't be the same without Michael,' she said.

Mabel's face brightened. She loved hearing about Michael. 'Show me his letter again,' she begged.

'Mabs! I showed you this morning.'

Mabel wriggled in her chair. 'I know. But I can't believe he mentioned *me*!'

Helen gave her a hard stare and said, in Miss Thomas's voice, 'I would be very disappointed to see signs of Unbecoming Conduct in Collegiate girls.'

They both giggled as Helen slipped the letter out of the book George had lent her, leaving it sitting on the table. Of course she would never normally let anyone read a private letter, but Michael had specifically asked to be remembered to Mabel:

> *How's your pal Mabel? We've some greedy lads here must never have had a square meal till they joined the army but I still say I've never seen anyone eat ice cream like her. Tell her that from me.*

'Cheeky!' Mabel said, digging her spoon deep into her sundae dish, and blushing. 'What else does he say?' She moved round beside Helen so they could look together, and her soft dark hair tickled Helen's cheek.

I don't mind telling you we are all fed up with being stuck in camp, still in Ireland, training training training; drilling drilling drilling. And some of the fellows training us – well, I don't think they can be the cream of the regiment, otherwise they'd be off doing some real soldiering, wouldn't they? Not trying to lick us into shape. But the good news is, we are to be posted soon – within a fortnight I think. Can't wait for some real action. So soon I'll be writing to you from France. Maybe I'll even run into the bold Sandy out there – wouldn't that be a joke?

'That's all.' Helen folded the letter and slid it back into its envelope. She picked up *The Men of '98* to put it inside.

'What's that?' Mabel asked. 'Lessons?'

'George Rae lent it to me. It's about the United Irishmen and the 1798 rebellion.'

'Sounds boring. Or are you just pretending to read it to impress George?'

'Of course not,' Helen said. 'And if I was, it's better than impressing a boy with your ice-cream-eating ability.'

Mabel giggled and sucked the last bit of yellow ice cream from her spoon. Then she became serious.

'Has Michael made up with his family yet?' she asked.

'Not exactly.' *Soon*, Helen thought, *when I've delivered the letter.*

Mabel put her hand on her chest in a dramatic gesture. 'Imagine! The prodigal son!'

'Mabs? I hope you're not getting a bit Florence Bell-ish over this?'

'What do you mean?'

'Turning it into a romantic story. Because it really isn't.' For the first time in ages she thought of the night Michael had crashed into their house, drunk and bleeding. 'It isn't romantic at all.'

17.

Was any day ever as long as Good Friday? Helen lay back in the hay and looked out at the farmyard from the open shed. Nothing stirred. Fly dozed at her kennel door, head on her paws. All the animals were out in the fields. Papa had taken Uncle Sean's bicycle and set off to visit an old teaching pal in Newcastle.

It was last year's hay, dry and dusty, but it still made a soft if tickly bed. Helen had collected the eggs for Aunt Bridie, and been for a walk over the mountain, where the golden whins, smelling of coconut, glowed against a pewter sky. Fly had looked up when Helen called her and then let her grizzled head sink back onto her paws, so she had gone alone. *If I were Florence Bell*, Helen thought, *I would say that dog's pining for Michael.* She had been reading *The New Girl at St Chad's* for hours. Since Miss Thomas had banned Angela Brazil's school stories, they had become all the rage with the lower fourth. It was a bit daft: Helen didn't know why all Irish girls in English school stories had to be wild and rebellious. *She* wasn't wild at all – but perhaps that was because she wasn't a proper Irish girl. Still, *The New Girl at St. Chad's* was more readable than the book about that rebellion that George had lent her.

The kitten she had cuddled at new year was nowhere to be seen, but there was a new one, almost identical, only with a splodge of ginger on its white nose, to which Helen had completely given her heart, and it lay in the hay beside her, cleaning its face.

She was hungry, but there would be fish for tea, because it was Friday, and fish always made her feel sick. She hoped Mama wouldn't make her eat it. In the corner of the barn she could see the pen that Michael and Sandy had made for the injured calf, empty now. She wondered if the calf had recovered. She had wanted to ask Uncle Sean but he had been so irritable she hadn't liked to. He was shorthanded on the farm without Michael, of course, and now Gerry wasn't around much because his mother was ill.

And Nora! Nora had been *hateful*. Maybe she missed Gerry too, but she didn't need to take it out on Helen. Treating her as if she were about ten. Lots of scornful, *Oh you wouldn't understand*s. That was why Helen hadn't given her the letter yet. She had enjoyed the thought of it hiding in her handkerchief box, in her suitcase under Nora's sagging bed. And Nora not knowing. Ha! She'd have given it to Aunt Bridie, but Michael had *said* to give it to Nora. And he'd said she would know the right time. It wasn't her fault if Nora was too mean to let there be a right time.

Fly lifted her head from her paws, as if she had heard something, and then let it sink down with a sigh, as Uncle Sean turned the corner into the yard, followed by Aunt Bridie, Nora and Mama, all in their Sunday best. Helen raced to meet them.

'Careful,' Mama said, when Helen took her arm. 'You shouldn't be tearing round like that on Good Friday.'

'I was lying in the hay, actually,' Helen said. 'Reading,' she went on, in case lying around was also something you shouldn't do on Good Friday.

'You have hayseed in your hair,' Nora said. She was wearing a pious expression and a mauve hat from which her dark hair peeped out very becomingly. She looked so pretty it made Helen fizz with jealousy.

Helen ran her hands through her hair – her plait had come undone and she felt unkempt beside all these Sunday-dressed people. She felt like she needed a good scratch.

'Was mass nice?' she asked.

'Not *mass*,' Nora said. 'Don't you know anything?'

Helen looked at Mama, confused.

Mama sighed. 'Well, it's not really the mass today. Good Friday is special. The ceremonies are different.'

'Is that why it takes so long?' Helen asked.

'We did the stations too,' Aunt Bridie said.

'Of the cross,' Nora said. She fingered the silver crucifix round her neck.

'I *know* what the stations are,' Helen lied. 'I'm not stupid.'

'And kissing the cross, of course.' Nora sighed beatifically. 'I love that: the whole parish queuing up to kiss the feet of Our Lord.'

Aunt Bridie sounded weary. 'Go on in and make some tea, girls. We'll be in in a minute.'

Helen trailed after Nora into the farmhouse kitchen.

'What's your book?' Nora asked, setting the big black kettle onto the range.

Wishing, after all, she could have shown off with *The Men of '98*, Helen held out *The New Girl at St Chad's*.

Nora wrinkled her nose. 'When *I* was at school,' she said, as if this was at least a decade ago, 'the nuns banned all school stories. *Especially* Angela Brazil. And I don't think you should be reading something so frivolous on Good Friday.'

If Helen had liked Nora or if she hadn't had such a lonely afternoon, she might have admitted that Miss Thomas banned them too, and they might have compared notes about their dragon schoolmarms. Maybe they would even have had a giggle together, and Helen might have lent Nora the book when she was finished. And then given her the letter. But because Nora sounded so superior, Helen tossed her head, getting a mouthful of hair and hayseed, and said, 'It was a lot more fun than sitting in a stupid church all afternoon anyway.'

Nora stretched her eyes wide in exaggerated horror. 'Good Friday isn't meant to be *fun*. It's the most solemn day of the year. But when you've been raised as a *heathen* –'

'Take that back! I go to church every week,' Helen said. 'And at least' – with a sudden memory of what Nora had said about kissing the cross – '*we* don't worship graven images. Kissing the cross? Goodness knows what you could catch.'

Nora gasped. '*Catch*? From the feet of Our Lord? How could you even *say* that? You don't know what you're talking about, you baby, with your Angela Brazil and your –'

'*If* I were a baby,' Helen said very coolly, '*Michael* wouldn't be writing to me every week, would he? Telling me all about the army? He doesn't write to *you*, does he?'

She turned to stalk out, but Nora rushed at her, grabbed her loose hair, yanked hard. Helen screamed, snatched at the front of Nora's stupid blouse. The little silver chain broke, and crucifix and chain slithered to the stone-flagged floor.

'Girls!' Aunt Bridie stood in the doorway, her hands on her hips. 'Fighting! On Good Friday of all days.'

'It was her,' Nora wailed, her breath whooshing down her nose. 'Look!' She bent down and lifted the broken chain.

'She attacked me.' Helen rubbed her burning scalp.

'Both of you – upstairs. Now.'

When Aunt Bridie spoke like that you obeyed. Nora stomped ahead, her bun of dark hair gleaming. How annoying that Helen hadn't had a chance to pull that smug bun hard!

'You're not coming in *my* room,' Nora said.

'I wouldn't want to. It stinks.'

Nora slammed her door behind her, and Helen hesitated on the landing. Apart from Nora's room, and Aunt Bridie and Uncle Sean's, there was one proper guest room where Mama and Papa were sleeping, and Michael's little room. Dared she go in? It had never been suggested that she sleep there, even though it was empty, and she hated sharing Nora's lumpy, sweat-smelling bed. But she had an idea she would be in even more trouble if she went to sit in there. *I don't belong anywhere*, she thought tragically. *I want to go home.*

In the end she hunched herself into the tiny windowsill on the landing, and curled up, looking out at the still yard. Gerry, gangly, taller than Michael though he was only sixteen, with a shock of blond hair and a very holey green jersey, rode into the yard. He jumped off his bicycle and leaned it against the red barn door. He looked round – for Nora, maybe? – and then loped off towards the milking shed. *Ha,* thought Helen. *You won't find her.*

This was boring. Her book was downstairs, and she didn't dare go down for it. Even *The Men of '98* would have been better than nothing.

She could hear voices from downstairs. Mama: 'Helen must have provoked her. Goodness knows, she can be provoking enough.' *Thanks, Mama!*

And then Aunt Bridie: 'Just leave them to cool down. They're at that age. Nora's been very difficult since – well ... And I don't really like Gerry's influence.' She lowered her voice but Helen strained to hear. 'It's not just that he's only a farmhand. But he has her head turned about suffering Ireland. Since the Fianna started in the town he's got very radical ideas. I don't like it. I'm glad it wasn't going when Michael was that age – och, let's go and have some tea, Eileen. And then we'll walk down to the stream and pick some daffodils.'

She heard them go into the parlour and close the door. Uncle Sean, changed into his old cap, walked across the yard to get the cows down for milking. He whistled to Fly and she slunk along, weaving in and out of his legs like a black and white furry eel.

Gradually Helen became aware of another sound. A snuffling, breathy noise from behind Nora's door. Nora was crying.

And she called me *a baby!* Helen thought. *I'm the one had my hair practically trailed out by the roots, and I'm not crying! I'm the one banished to a cold landing with nothing to do except look out at a boring old farmyard. She's only looking for attention.* She held her breath and listened. There it was again: a tiny muffled sniff and a catching of breath. It wasn't attention-seeking crying at all. It was the kind of crying Helen couldn't ignore.

You did *break her chain*, she reminded herself.

She uncurled herself – her legs had gone numb and she had to give them a good rub.

'Nora?' she whispered at the white-painted door.

The sobbing stopped.

'Nora? Are you all right? Look, I – I've something to tell you.'

'G'way. I hate you, you Proddy British –'

'Good,' Helen said. 'Because I hate you too. And Michael hates you. *That's* what I was going to tell you. He loves being in the British army. He never wants to come back here. He never wants to see any of you again.'

18.

Helen was collecting the eggs on Easter Tuesday when the first news came about the Dublin uprising. It was Papa who brought it, rattling into the yard on Uncle Sean's bike, a newspaper clamped to the carrier above the back wheel.

'See this?' he said.

Helen gathered her basket under her arm. He showed her the front page: DUBLIN RIOTS! CITY UNDER SIEGE.

For a terrible moment Helen saw the word CITY and thought – *Belfast!* And her stomach squeezed tight, until she saw that it was only Dublin. A hundred miles away. Nothing to do with her.

She looked at the black-and-white grainy photo of a street in ruins, and then up at Papa's serious face.

'Who are they?' she asked. 'What do they want? Is it Home Rule?'

'A bit more than that.' Papa jabbed his finger on the page. 'They declared a republic yesterday. Madness! As if they've got a hope. Connolly and Pearse and – oh, a whole crowd of rebels. Taken over the city!'

'Papa! Mabel's in Dublin! Will she be all right?'

Papa frowned, then turned it into a smile. 'Och, sure to be. She probably doesn't even know there's anything happening. Remember when there was rioting in Belfast? You and Mama had no idea there was anything happening until I got home and told you? It'll be like that. Storm in a teacup. And,' he added, folding the paper and starting to walk towards the house, 'the army will soon put them down, that's for sure.'

★ ★ ★

Uncle Sean didn't share Papa's view that it was a storm in a teacup. He paced the kitchen as if he wanted to walk to Dublin and join in, his big face getting redder and redder.

'This is what we've been waiting for!' he said. 'An Irish republic.' And he said something in Irish which Helen didn't understand, and which made Papa twitch. 'It's a great day,' he said. 'Nora. Bridie. Remember this day. This is the birth of your nation.'

He didn't say anything about it being Helen's nation. He put an arm round his wife and his daughter, then looked round the kitchen, as if searching for someone. His eyes rested on the high corner shelf where Michael's hurling trophies still sat.

'Where's Gerry the day?' he asked. 'Gerry's a patriot. He'll be rejoicing at this.'

'Gerry has bigger things to worry him,' Aunt Bridie said. 'Theresa'll hardly last the week.'

'There's *nothing* bigger than being a patriot!' Nora cried.

'Nora! God forgive you,' Aunt Bridie said. 'I hope you're remembering that poor woman in your prayers.'

'It's not really a republic, is it?' Papa cut in. 'Just because some rebels say it is, and raise a home-made flag? I wouldn't call it more than just another riot. Goodness knows, we've had plenty of those. North *and* south.'

Helen looked at the paper. She didn't really want to – the news was all of barricaded streets and looting and snipers – the city seemed to have gone mad. Some of the photos looked exactly like photos she had seen of ruined cities on the Front. In Sandy's last letter he had said they were billeted in a town where there wasn't a single roof left. They'd had to fix tarpaulins up to keep the rain out.

Mama shook her head. 'As if there's not enough fighting in France.'

'Their poor mothers,' Aunt Bridie said.

And Helen knew in that moment that she must give Aunt Bridie Michael's letter. *Now*. Never mind what Michael had said about giving it to Nora. Nora, who thought there was nothing bigger than being a patriot.

But – oh dear. This was the very opposite of the right time.

'Their mothers should be proud of them!' Nora said.

Uncle Sean nodded. 'We've waited long enough for this, daughter. I wish' – he hesitated. He hadn't spoken Michael's name in the house for weeks – 'I could think of *my* son down there in Dublin, there, fighting for his nation.'

'Michael *is* fighting for his nation,' Papa said quietly. 'Much more effectively than these eejits occupying post offices and – and biscuit factories.' He made it sound ridiculous. 'I'd be proud of him if he were my son.'

'Och, we know *you* would be! If it hadn't been for you –'

'Sean,' Aunt Bridie said warningly.

'My friend Mabel's in Dublin,' Helen said in a small voice, in an attempt at distraction.

'Lucky her,' Nora said. It was the first time she had spoken to Helen, even indirectly, since Good Friday. Which was extremely awkward, since they still had to share a bed. 'I wish I was there, watching history being made. And I know Gerry'll be mad to be missing out.' Her cheeks burned and her eyes blazed.

Helen felt, once again, as ignorant as a kitten. *Was* history being made? Or were a few hotheads and eejits just causing trouble? Was it brave of the rebels to stand up for what they believed in – or wrong to take the law into their own hands? Were they patriots or traitors? The paper had said they were being helped by Germany. Surely that was treason?

'The army will soon sort them out,' Papa said. 'It's a scandal, of course, to distract them from fighting the Hun – but it can't last long.

'That's the whole idea!' Uncle Sean said. And he banged his fist so hard on the wooden table that the blue and white dish of eggs wobbled and danced, and Aunt Bridie had to put her hand on it to steady it. 'England's difficulty is Ireland's opportunity. A nation once again!'

'There'll be no republic,' Papa said. 'And whatever madness happens in Dublin – this is Ulster. Loyal to the crown.'

Uncle Sean huffed. 'And this is *my house*.' He raised himself up and rocked back on his heels. He was much bigger than Papa.

'James,' Aunt Bridie said very quietly, 'I think maybe you'd all be happier in your own home.'

19.

All the way home on the train, dozing against her father's shoulder and trying to ignore her growing queasiness – she didn't normally get train-sick; it was just nerves – Helen worried that somehow, when they got home, Belfast would have changed, the rioting would have spread, the streets would be burning as they were in Dublin. She kept looking at her suitcase above her in the rack, thinking of the letter still there in the handkerchief box. She should have found a way to give it to Aunt Bridie. Probably she could have. But she hadn't. Sending them home like that! *Aunt Bridie!*

The station at Queen's Quay looked as usual, apart from a large sign saying NO TRAINS TO/FROM DUBLIN UNTIL FURTHER NOTICE.

Helen turned her face away from the newsstand and blocked her ears to the cry of 'Tele! Latest on the Dublin riots!' from the paperboy in the street. On the tram, people were talking about it – the general feeling being that the army would soon sort everything out – but other than that, Belfast was its own familiar self. Cyclamen Terrace had never looked so welcoming.

'Can I run round to see if Mabel's safely home?' Helen begged when they had brought everything in, and Mama had made some tea.

'Of course not! Don't be silly,' Mama said.

'But Mama!'

'I could walk round with her, Eileen,' Papa said quietly. 'It's only natural that she's worried.'

'Mabel won't be home – you saw the signs in the station as well as I did,' Mama said. 'She's probably enjoying an extra few days' holiday with her aunt.'

'Oh, Mama, *please*!' Helen begged. 'I won't be able to sleep. At least Mabel's mother might have some news of her.' She didn't see how: the pictures she had seen of Dublin were terrible – bicycles and bedsteads barricading the streets; buildings smouldering for all the world as if they were in France. But surely if anything terrible had happened to Mabel – she would *know*. Somehow. But then she had always believed she would know if something bad happened to Sandy. And while he'd been having his arm sewn back together in a field hospital she'd been playing hockey for the fourth eleven against Victoria College and hadn't had the remotest inkling.

'You don't deserve a treat, young lady,' Mama said. 'I haven't forgotten the disgraceful way you and Nora behaved.'

But Papa said, 'Well, I want to call on Mother and Violet – make sure things are all right with them after the holiday. It's not out of the way to go via Mabel's house. Go on, Helen – run and fetch your hat.'

Mama's mouth got very tight, exactly the way Aunt Violet's did.

But in the end there was no answer from Mabel's house at all. So Helen still didn't know what had happened. And Aunt Violet wanted to talk in tones of great outrage about the riots, and Granny was lying down with a headache, and Helen had to sit being seen and not heard in Aunt Violet's parlour for what felt like hours while Aunt Violet talked about how unpatriotic the rebels were. There was a new letter from Sandy and she insisted on reading it aloud. There was no mention of roofless houses or dead comrades. Certainly no mention of rum.

He's protecting her, Helen thought, watching Aunt Violet's chin bob with indignation as she compared Sandy and his men to the Dublin rebels. *I'm glad – mostly – that he doesn't need to protect me.*

'Taking troops away from where they're needed!' Aunt Violet kept saying. 'If Sandy and his brave loyal boys are the least bit compromised because of men being diverted to deal with that – that *rabble* …'

Helen wished she had stayed at home.

MAY 1916

20.

The rebellion seemed – as far as Helen could see – to be over by the weekend.

Papa's *News Letter* said that the uprising was contained, crushed by the might of the British army. The leaders had surrendered and would be 'dealt with'. Helen couldn't help shivering at that. It sounded sinister. She thought of Sandy's young Private C and how he had been *dealt with*. But that had been for cowardice. Surely the leaders in Dublin had been the opposite of cowards? Misguided, maybe even treacherous, as Papa believed – but surely, in their own way – *brave*?

She didn't say this to anyone at home or school.

Papa was satisfied that the army had dealt so effectively with the situation.

'After all,' he said, 'they've held the German line since 1914 – they were hardly going to be bested by a few Sinn Féin rebels, were they?'

'I suppose not,' Helen said.

By the time the trains were running properly, Mabel had to start term a day or so late, but with no very exciting story after all.

'We just couldn't go out,' she said, riffling through the books in her locker. 'Oh, *where's* that pigging algebra book hiding itself? Aunt Jean was terrified. We had to stay in the house for the whole week, waiting for it to be over. And we got awfully hungry. So much for tea at the Shelbourne! We had stale bread and stuff from tins.

There was nothing in the shops, and Aunt Jean wouldn't even let me walk to the end of the road to see what was going on. Sometimes you could hear the fighting in the distance,' she said, her eyes going big and round, 'but mostly it was just boring.'

'So it wasn't like seeing history being made?' Helen thought of how Nora's eyes had gleamed during that awful row.

Mabel shrugged. 'Not really. But it was horrible – on the way to the station, seeing the streets all wrecked and smouldering. I was very glad to get home. I don't fancy going to Dublin ever again. Ah!' She pounced on a small blue book. 'There you are, you rotten thing.'

Even Sandy's next letter mentioned the rebellion:

> *The Germans have got wind of it and they've been taunting us – saying the British army is killing our wives and children on the streets of Dublin. Which is nonsense of course – this is an Ulster regiment, but I don't suppose they know the difference. All the same, I wouldn't have liked to be sent to Dublin. I never thought I'd be glad to be over here in a trench but at least we know what we're up against.*

At school Dr Allen preached about patriotism and the coming exams. Some of their old boys, now in the Officers' Training Corps at Trinity College in Dublin, had been involved in defending Trinity against the rebels, and had promised a story for the next edition of the school magazine.

'Bags me edit that when it comes in,' George Rae said.

'If Helen doesn't mind,' Edith said.

Helen shook her head. She was shy with Edith now, not sure how to treat her after her brother's death. She didn't want to make the kind of sickly fuss Florence made, but it seemed mean not to say *something*. But she hadn't found the right words the first time Edith had come back to the magazine committee and now the time had passed.

'He's welcome to it,' Helen said.

Now that it was all over she didn't want to hear another word about burning streets and barricades and people getting killed. It had all been just a bit too close for comfort.

And it was about to get very much closer still.

21.

'Has Michael gone to France yet?' Mabel asked as they walked home from the tram stop together on Friday.

Helen shook her head. 'Haven't heard from him since that letter I showed you before Easter.'

'That's strange.'

Helen frowned. 'You always used to ask about *Sandy*,' she said, to take the conversation away from Michael and letters. What if Michael were already in France and his family didn't even know? But after that awful row she didn't see how she would ever have another chance to deliver his letter. She had thought of simply posting it, but what if Uncle Sean really did throw it in the fire? If anything happened to Michael that letter would be all they had of him. The best thing she could do for now was keep it safe.

'I haven't forgotten Sandy!' Mabel said. 'How is he?'

'He's all right. Says it's quieter where they are just now. I sent him the school magazine last week. I knew he'd be sorry about Hugh Hamilton – Sandy was friendly with his brother.'

Mabel looked serious for a moment, then sighed. 'Oh, I *wish* I had handsome cousins in the army. *My* cousins are all still at the toddling stage – all drool and sticky hands.'

'Well, at least the war'll be over before they're grown up,' Helen said. 'Come on – let's cut through the park.'

The early May evenings were warm. Helen sat at her window and looked over at the park, where drifts of bluebells lay under the huge oaks. She could imagine how cool and scented it must be, away from the dusty street. She was trying to make herself read the paper. All week the authorities in Dublin had been executing the leaders of the rising, the eighth one that morning. It was grim reading: name upon name of men – some Helen had heard of; most she hadn't – shot dead. After a while she tossed the paper aside, looked longingly at the Angela Brazil Mabel had lent her, *The Fortunes of Philippa*, but then made herself tackle her French prep. Papa had gone to a meeting at the church; Mama was lying down. She had been coughing again since Easter, but Helen knew better than to suggest her going to Derryward.

Helen leaned her forehead against the cold glass. If she sneaked out to the park, would Mama know? Prep on top of the newspaper stories was making her brain ache. *If* she ever went to college she would have to work like this all the time. Would it be worth it? Would she understand things better, or would it be all French verbs and Latin declensions? She thought of Uncle Sean and Papa shouting at each other about Ireland and Ulster and freedom and loyalty. It would take more than a college degree to help her make sense of all that. She sighed and went back to work. The ink in her pen had dried while she'd been looking out the window. She shook it, and ink spattered all over her French verbs.

'Bother!' She pushed the book away in disgust.

The whirr of a bicycle made her look out again. The telegraph boy. She held her breath as he cycled past their house and on down Cyclamen Terrace. Where was he going? She didn't know all the neighbours but the Thompsons at number 37 had a father at the Front; and the McVeas at number 43 two sons.

She strained to see where the boy would stop, following his progress down the street. He didn't stop at 37. He rode on past 43, stopped and talked to a soldier coming in the opposite direction, then turned the corner into Park Street and was gone. Helen transferred her attention to the soldier. He was too young to be Mr Thompson, and not tall enough for one of the lanky McVeas. He must be coming home on leave, because he carried a bag over his shoulder. He was stooped and tired-looking, like Sandy when he had first come home on sick leave, so that as he came closer she saw mostly the top of his cap. But there was something familiar in his gait, and when he drew close to the gate of number 22, he slowed down and looked up at her window.

It was Michael.

22.

'You stopped writing.'

It was hard not to sound accusatory. For ages she had worried, thought he might have been sent to France without her knowing, could even be in danger, and here he was, not a bother on him, turned up – again – on the doorstep. Only this time, at least he was sober. *More* than sober: his voice had a flatness she had never heard.

'Let's go out,' he had said, as soon as she had opened the door to him. 'I've been cooped up in a train for hours.'

Maybe, she thought, *he's only tired from travelling*, but a worm of unease started to twist in her stomach.

'I *couldn't* write,' he said, when they had turned off the street and into the park. 'I was busy.'

'You were never too busy before.' Helen ran her hand along the railings.

'I – last week …' Michael shook his head. 'I was …' He looked up at the trees, at the quiet terraced street on the other side of the railings. 'It's all so normal,' he said. 'I can't believe it.'

'It's the same as always,' Helen said. 'Why wouldn't it be?'

'Last week,' Michael said, still in that flat tone. 'I couldn't write because I was on – on active service.'

Helen jerked up her chin in surprise. 'You haven't been to the Front already?' But no, of course not; he wouldn't have been given leave so soon. Besides, he didn't have the look of someone who had been in France. And yet – she looked more closely. His face was thin, his eyes strained. In the three months since she had seen him he seemed to have aged three years or more.

'Not exactly.' He pulled a handful of leaves from a tree and started to shred them, systematically.

'Where then?'

'Dublin.'

Uncle Sean's voice boomed into her head. The day they had first heard of what Papa called the riots and he called the rising. 'I wish I could think of my son down there fighting for Ireland.' And all the time Michael had been –

'Michael?' she said stupidly. 'What were you – you weren't one of the rebels, were you?'

Michael gave a harsh laugh and indicated his uniform. 'Dressed like this?' he said. 'Hardly. But I – maybe I should have been.'

'You mean you were –'

'We were sent to restore order,' Michael said. 'There we were, trained and ready to go, and only thirty miles away. God! To think I couldn't wait for action. I didn't expect to get it on the streets of Dublin. I didn't think I'd be asked to kill my fellow Irishmen.'

He looked up, and his face was fierce.

'I'm never going back, Helen,' he said. 'I'm never going to follow orders like that again.'

'What do you mean?' The worm of unease buried itself deeper.

'I've deserted.'

23.

The most important thing was to make Michael change his mind.

'They'll shoot you. *Your own comrades* will shoot you. That's what happens. You must *know* that.' She yanked at a dandelion.

'They'll have to find me first,' Michael said. He glanced behind him as if the entire British army might be hiding in the park.

'Well, they won't have to look very hard, will they? You've come to one of the most obvious places.'

Her voice sounded calm – she sounded, she realised, just like Aunt Violet in one of her most bossy moods, but inside she was panicking. Her knowledge of what happened to deserters came entirely from that terrible letter from Sandy. The fate of Private C had haunted her, and lately had been mixed up with the news of the executions in Dublin. Wasn't desertion a kind of treason?

'So did you just run away?' she asked.

They were walking along the formal path lined with primroses, watching the setting sun warm up the red brick of Cyclamen Terrace.

Maybe he could run back again? Surely it would be different since they weren't at the Front? But she knew the army didn't let you away with it. Would *she* get into trouble, for aiding and abetting a deserter? He must go back! But then – *could* you just return to the army as if nothing had happened?

'I'm on leave. They've given us four days and then – off to France.'

Relief flooded her. 'So nobody knows you've – I mean that you're thinking of –'

'I won't turn up for the draft,' he said, as if this were something simple. As if it weren't something to be deeply ashamed of.

She thought of the day they had seen Sandy off. *Sandy* knew how bad war could be. He had already been out there and proved himself, and nearly lost his arm. Sandy admitted, even if only to her, that it was hard, and yet he had never – not for a moment – contemplated not turning up. Not turning up was for cowards. And Michael had had such a tiny taste of war – squashing a few rebels on the streets of Dublin! It hardly compared with what her brave Sandy had done! How awful, to be feeling so – ashamed of him!

And then she was ashamed of herself. For *she* had been a coward – maybe worse than a coward – in not delivering that letter. But she couldn't think about that now. She had to be practical.

'How long have you got?' she asked. 'I mean – when are you supposed to report back?'

'Tuesday night,' he said. 'I don't know where I'll –'

'It's all right,' she said. 'You can stay with us – didn't Mama and Papa say you must think of our house as home?'

Somehow, while he stayed at Cyclamen Terrace, he must be persuaded not to desert.

She patted his rough khaki sleeve. 'And don't worry about anything else until you have to.'

She couldn't believe how grown-up she sounded, and Michael must have thought so too because he smiled for the first time and said, 'Thanks, Helen. I knew I could rely on you.'

Helen couldn't meet his eyes. 'It's getting chilly,' she said after a moment. 'Let's go inside.'

'I'm not telling your parents what I've been doing,' Michael said, as they turned into the gateway of number 22. 'So don't ask me.'

'But Papa will be so proud of you!' Helen said without thinking.

Michael gave a brief, bitter laugh. 'Well, that makes one of us,' he said. 'If you tell them, I'll leave. I won't wait till Tuesday.'

Her parents were surprised to see Michael but made him welcome. Mama even bustled about, getting him some supper. But when he sat down at the dainty tray, with an egg and some of Granny's fruit loaf, he set down his knife and said, 'I'm sorry. I don't seem to be hungry after all. Would you mind if I just went to bed?'

And he heaved himself up the stairs like an old man.

Papa looked after him and frowned. 'He doesn't look well, does he? Exhausted.'

'Well, I suppose the training must be quite hard,' Mama said, 'if they're to make them ready to fight.'

'For a strong farm lad like that?' Papa sounded sceptical. 'He looks like he's sickening for something.'

'I hope not,' Mama said. 'That's all we need.'

'Did he say anything to you, Helen?' Papa asked.

Helen shook her head. 'Nothing much.'

24.

Saturday was another bright spring day, and Mama suggested that Helen take Michael for a walk by the Lagan. 'Put some colour in your cheeks,' she said.

Michael said he didn't mind, so they took the tram up the Malone Road, and walked down a winding lane, past big grand houses and a few old cottages. They passed a couple of factory girls, walking arm in arm, who goggled at them. Michael looked down at his uniform as if it disgusted him. *But at least,* Helen thought, *he is still wearing it.* Perhaps now he had had a night's sleep he would give up the ridiculous idea of desertion.

'It's hard to believe we're still in the city, isn't it?' Helen said, stopping to talk to a grey donkey in a field. It stuck its nose through the fence and nuzzled at her dress, leaving behind a trail of green slobber.

'Yes,' Michael said. 'I've had enough of city streets.'

That was all he said until they were walking by the river. Helen tried various conversation openings – Sandy's last letter; Mabel's adventures in Dublin – but Michael just said yes or no. Maybe they weren't the most tactful of subjects, but it was so wearing. It was, in fact, very like when Sandy had first come home from hospital.

And then, along the tow path, watching the slow brown river nose past, with the trees on the opposite bank bent down into frondy caves, he suddenly said, 'I'd never even been to Dublin before.'

'Me neither.'

'I always wanted to see it. Da was there once and he always talked about it being the glorious capital of a free Ireland one day. Christ! It doesn't look too glorious now.'

Helen was silent, scared to say the wrong thing.

'We spent weeks digging trenches and practising with bayonets and – it was all useless. All that teaching us to hate the Hun.' He pulled at a frond of bracken. 'I'd rather have been in the muckiest shell-hole on the Western Front than fighting in the streets of my own homeland,' he said quietly.

Easy to say, thought Helen, *when you've never been hear a mucky shell-hole.* And then she remembered Sandy's last letter: 'I never thought I'd be glad to be over here in a trench but at least we know what we're up against.'

'It was hell,' he said.

His voice shivered and when Helen looked at him she thought there were tears in his eyes. It reminded her of the night he had run away to join up. But he had been drunk then; he was definitely sober now.

'Tell me,' she said.

He shook his head and bit down hard on his bottom lip. 'It's too terrible. You'll hate me. I hate myself.'

She drew herself up to her full height. 'I'm not a child, you know. Sandy tells me things. Things he wouldn't tell Aunt Violet. I asked him to. I want to help.'

Michael sighed. 'You won't want to hear what I've done.'

She put her hand on his arm, feeling the rough wool of his uniform. 'You did what you had to do.' She thought of Sandy, giving the evidence which led to C's death. 'That's what people have to do in wars.'

Why had she not been able to think of those words back when Sandy might have needed to hear them?

'But that wasn't the war I signed up for!' he cried. 'I signed up to help fight Germany! To make the war end faster so that Ireland could claim her birthright – to help hold the line –'

'"Wherever it extends",' Helen finished for him. Even she knew that speech of Redmond's, the Nationalist leader. 'Well, last week the line extended to Dublin,' she went on. 'After all, you couldn't just sit back and let the rebels *attack* you.' Remembering something she had heard Aunt Violet say, she added, 'With their Hun guns!'

Michael gave a hoarse laugh. 'There's plenty of Hun guns up here in loyal Ulster,' he said. 'And yes – they *were* attacking us, Helen, because we were the *enemy*. *I* was suddenly the enemy of men I was brought up to revere! My family's heroes.' He groaned. 'It was chaos. Lewis – our officer – he hadn't a clue. This wasn't what he'd been trained for either. You didn't know where they were going to be shooting from – from roofs, out of windows, behind you, in front of you. Sometimes we were shooting blind, just vaguely in the right direction. We weren't in control. Not the way we'd been trained.' He rubbed his hand over his mouth. 'And you didn't know who was a rebel and who was just – just a person out on the streets.'

Helen remained quiet, her hand still on his arm.

'We were on this street,' he said. 'It was barricaded with all sorts of rubbish – bicycles – there was one the same as Da's; I kept thinking, what's my da's bicycle doing here? – and bedsteads, old fireplaces – I don't know how they got fireplaces into the streets, maybe I dreamt that? – and this kid started running at us. He was carrying something. Lewis said, "Get him; he's armed." And I yelled back, "He's only a kid, sir." And Lewis said, "Shoot him, damn you, or I'll shoot you."' He broke off, swallowed.

'So I shot him,' he said. His hand shook.

'You had to,' Helen reassured him. Her voice was strong but her heart hammered and she remembered Michael's hands gentling the injured calf at new year, settling it so carefully on its straw bed. They hadn't shaken then. 'You were obeying orders. He'd have shot you quick enough.'

'No. He wouldn't. He couldn't.' Michael's voice was so thick that Helen had to strain to hear him. 'When we got to him and rolled him over, it wasn't a gun he had at all. It was a bottle of ginger-beer. That's what he was "armed" with, Helen. And I *killed* him. He was lying in a pool of blood and ginger-beer and broken glass. He was only about ten.'

Helen thought of the mutilated lamb.

Michael looked into the river for a long time. 'I didn't sign up to kill Irishmen,' he said, 'and I certainly didn't sign up to kill children.'

His eyes were screwed shut. 'Every time I close my eyes I see his face.' He shuddered. 'I can't sleep for seeing him. I can't eat. I feel sick all the time.' He opened his eyes and looked straight ahead of him at the slow brown river. 'What am I going to do?' he asked. 'I wish – oh God, I wish I could go home.'

And to Helen's horror, he started to cry, proper tearing sobs, like a girl. Not like a soldier at all. She wanted to run from his pain as she had run from the lamb – it was too raw, and too frightening. But she didn't.

She tightened her hand on his arm and said, 'Michael – you *should* go home. You need to be with your family.'

And this is too big for me.

He turned to look at her, his face marbled with tears. 'I can't,' he choked out. 'Remember the letter? – well, of course you do; you delivered it.' He snapped a twig between his fingers, and when he spoke again his voice was calmer. 'I asked them, *if* they forgave me, *if* I was still their son, to write to me at the camp. But' – his mouth twisted – 'not a word. So I know, don't I? They don't forgive me and I can't go home. Ever.'

His voice cracked, and he put his hand over hers, and she threaded her fingers in his, but could think of nothing to say.

'The morning we were deployed,' he said, 'that was the day I gave up hope. I'd lost my family to join the army, and then, when they sent us out to kill Irishmen in our own country – well, it was like I'd lost the army too. Like there was *nothing* left.' Before she could say anything, he went on, 'So you see why I have to desert?'

'But you'll get yourself killed. Or locked up.'

'Maybe I should be locked up,' Michael said.

'Don't be daft. You have your whole life ahead of you.' Despite the uniform, and being almost five years older than her, Michael seemed suddenly very young. 'But *not* if you get arrested for desertion.'

'So I'll go on the run,' he said as if this were a sensible solution.

'Don't be stupid. What kind of life is that?' Her voice was shrill with worry.

Michael squeezed her hand and said, 'Och, Helen, I'm sorry. I shouldn't have worried you with all this. It's not fair. But you're the only one I can trust, and –'

Trust. She looked into the brown Lagan and wondered how it was possible to feel this guilty.

'Michael,' she said. 'Maybe you *can* go home. You see, they haven't ignored you.' She swallowed. 'It was me. I – I didn't give them the letter.'

25.

She cried much more than Michael had, her face a mess of tears and snuffles. Michael was staring at her in disbelief, or disgust, his face a mask she couldn't read – set and tight, paler than she had ever seen it, his eyes burning black. He no longer seemed very young.

'I trusted you,' he said. 'You *asked* me to trust you. It was all your idea!'

'I – I know,' she whispered. 'I'm so sor–'

'Don't!' he shouted.

He sounded like Uncle Sean, and she stepped back. Spit bloomed in the corners of his lips. She had never been frightened of her cousin before but she was frightened now.

'You're just a stupid wee girl,' he said. Then, stumbling against a tree as he did so, he turned and walked away.

26.

Michael's place at the table stayed empty, the white linen napkin rolled into its little silver ring. Mama and Papa quizzed her.

'He can't just have wandered off and left you on the riverbank? On your *own*? We only let you go with him because we thought he'd look after you.'

'I don't need to be looked after,' she muttered, stabbing her fork into her cutlet.

She couldn't eat a thing. There was ginger-beer for a treat. She took one sip, remembered, gagged and set the glass down. She thought of Michael sitting at this table last night, staring at the food. Her eyes filled with tears and she blinked them back.

'You're fourteen and you're a girl,' Mama said. 'We trusted Michael to take care of you! It's the least he could do, after we've welcomed him into our home!'

Trust.

'Was he ill, or – or upset?' Papa asked. 'He didn't seem his usual self last night.'

Helen hesitated. 'I don't think he was ill,' she said honestly. 'But yes – maybe upset.'

'He'll need to take himself in hand before he goes to France on Tuesday.' Mama shook her head.

'Could he have gone home?' Papa suggested. 'I know things were difficult – but surely, if he's going abroad next week, they'd all be prepared to let bygones be bygones? After all he could –' He left the sentence unfinished but Helen added the words in her head, *he could be killed.*

Not if he doesn't go, she argued to herself. But that wasn't true, was it? If he didn't go, he was just as likely to be killed.

And it was her fault.

What can I do? she thought. *If I tell my parents how mean I've been they'll be shocked. And it won't do any good. They won't let me do anything about it. The letter. I have to deliver the letter. Now. And then – well, somehow we have to find him, and make him change his mind.*

She didn't know how she would do the second of those things. But she could surely get herself to Derryward.

It was the last place in the world she felt like going. Just remembering the last time she was there made her skin burn.

But it was the only way she could put things right.

She couldn't just say, 'Oh, by the way, I'm going off on my own to Derryward this afternoon. I'm going to get the train alone and then somehow get from the station to the farm.'

Maybe it would be enough to tell Papa – not Mama; Mama would be horrified – and he could go with her to Deryward, explain for her. In her imagination she saw her father's kind, stern face, heard his voice explaining how it wasn't her fault, how Michael shouldn't have expected her to do such a thing.

And then disgust crept down her neck. Michael had only done what she asked him to. 'You're just a wee girl,' he'd said. She squared her shoulders.

'Is it all right if I go round to Mabel's?' she asked. 'She wants us to practise tennis.'

'You were out all morning,' Mama objected, but Papa said, 'Och, Eileen, let her. The good weather is to break soon and she'll be cooped up.'

Helen dashed up to her room and found the letter. She put it carefully in her school satchel, and added all the money she had; a handkerchief; a book for the train – she didn't think she could concentrate on reading, but it was a long way, and if someone tried to speak to her, then she could pretend to read and hopefully they would ignore her. She dithered about *The Men of '98* – but it was tough going and besides, was it the sort of book she should be reading in public? It was terribly respectable of course – nothing so dull could be anything else – but someone could see it and get the wrong idea. She thought of the boy Michael had shot in Dublin. She grabbed *The Fortunes of Philippa* but then set it down again. No. This was a grown-up mission, and she wasn't going to look like a silly little girl. Instead she looked at the six Jane Austens she had been given for Christmas, fat red editions with the titles in gold, and picked up *Emma,* which she had started and abandoned because she thought she ought to tackle *The Men of '98.*

She checked her money – it wasn't enough for a return fare. Where in the house could she find some cash? Mama and Papa weren't the sort to leave it lying around. And besides, she didn't think she should add stealing to her crimes.

Mabel! Mabel still had the birthday money she had saved for Dublin and been unable to spend. And setting off down the street towards Mabel's house gave verisimilitude to the story that she was going there to play tennis. She added her racquet to the satchel – she could leave it at Mabel's; she needn't cart it the whole way to Derryward.

At the last minute, she scribbled a note.

Dear Michael, I am so sorry. I know that's just a word, but I have gone to deliver your letter now. I know I should have done it weeks ago. Please don't do anything foolish. Helen

She had been about to write 'desert' after 'Please don't', but then she wondered who might read this note if Michael didn't, so she changed it.

She put it in one of the envelopes Aunt Violet had given her for Christmas, wrote 'Michael' on it, and then added 'Private' and left it on her desk. *It's as if I'm running away,* she thought. The girls in her school stories were always running away, but usually because they had been Wrongfully Accused.

She had been Rightfully Accused.

She just caught Mabel; the whole family was on their way to the Botanic Gardens for an outing. Mabel was horrified at the story Helen told her, and at her plans.

'All the way down there? On the train? On your *own*? Won't you be terrified?'

'Yes,' Helen admitted. 'But I have to go, Mabs. It's the only way to put things right.'

'You could post the letter. They'd get it in a day or two.'

'I did think of that. But a day or two could be too late. And what if it got lost? Or ended up in the fire?'

'I think you're crazy,' Mabel said, 'but I'd come with you if I could.'

'I know you would.' Helen looked down at the ten-shilling note Mabel had given her. 'I'll pay you back,' she said.

'Doesn't matter.'

They hugged, and then Helen set off on the longest journey she had ever taken on her own.

27.

Helen stood in the middle of the bustling station, jumping at the shrieks of the whistle, and pulled her bag closer to her. She had never been anywhere like this alone before. It was nothing like getting the tram to school every day, or adventuring to Caprini's with Mabel. It was much scarier than getting the tram home alone from Malone, and that had seemed an adventure at the time. Only a couple of hours ago.

But it was *nothing* compared to what Sandy had been doing for over a year. She set her jaw and joined one of the ticket queues.

The man at the desk looked at her strangely when she asked for a half-fare day return.

'My mother's just –' Helen indicated vaguely behind her. 'She thought the other queue was shorter. We had a sort of argument about it.' She smiled widely.

He said nothing, except, 'Platform 2, ten past. Mind yourself now.'

She had almost expected the train to look monstrous, like a nightmare train, but of course it looked just as always. She found a corner seat and hoped nobody would sit beside her. She took out *Emma* and found the place where she had left off, but after a while she set it down and watched the endless red-brick terraces give way to the fields and drumlins of County Down. It was strange not to have Mama or Papa to point out landmarks too – the moment when they crossed the Lagan; the last house

142

in Belfast – they always argued over which actually was the last house – the two chocolate-brown donkeys in the field with the falling-down barn. She remembered the donkey they had seen that morning.

She was sure that old couple across the aisle were staring in disapproval – a young girl out on her own! They would know from her clothes she was a schoolgirl. Factory and mill girls her age could go out alone because, of course, they were sort of grown-ups, but even so, you didn't really see them alone, they were always with their pals. *I wish Mabel had come with me,* she thought, *but then what would she have done when I got there?* It was going to be hard enough, explaining, without an audience. Even though Mabel was the nicest girl in the world, she couldn't be expected to understand this kind of family hoo-ha. *George Rae would understand,* she thought suddenly. *Maybe one day I'll be able to tell him. Perhaps when I give him back* The Men of '98. Then she thought of how little she would like George to know what a beast she had been, and she sighed and looked back at *Emma*. Emma could be a bit of a beast too, but at least Jane Austen would make sure it all turned out all right in the end.

I don't know how this is going to turn out.

At Saintfield she looked out to see a soldier get out of the next carriage. He paused on the platform, looked round uncertainly, and then lifted his hand in greeting. A girl in a rust-coloured jacket ran to him, and when he took her in his arms her hat fell half-off. She had hair as red as Sandy's, all curls. As the train started huffing off again, Helen saw him take her hand.

By the time the train finally trundled into the little wayside station, Helen was ready to cry with tiredness, and dying to go to the lavatory. The station was too small to have a cloakroom. Never, never had she arrived alone. Never had Uncle Sean or Michael not been there with the mare and the trap. Nobody else got off here and she knew she had a long walk to the farm. At least she needn't go through the town – you could go that way, past the Gaelic Club and the chapel, and the square of shops and houses; it was a better road, but longer. But there was another way: you crossed the road outside the station, above the mill and the two big houses, and went only a little way up the hill, and then down a tiny road with whin and hawthorn hedges all along one side and the high grey wall of a big estate on the other. The son of the big house in there had been killed at Gallipoli, she remembered being told. The road was very rough: Uncle Sean always said it was hard on the mare's shoes – if she was going to pick up a stone it was always on that road.

After not very long Helen felt like she had stones in *her* shoes. And, oh, if she didn't go to the lavatory soon she would burst. The girls in books were always tramping over the hills for fun, and they *never* needed the lavatory, though they drank gallons of tea and lemonade. And they always found a smiling cottager selling teas or even ices to weary schoolgirls. There were several wayside cottages here, but their doors were shut. She wished for even a sip of the ginger-beer she had pushed aside at lunchtime. Well, maybe not ginger-beer. She tried walking on the other side of the road, in the shade of the wall, but then she was too cold.

Why had she never noticed before how steep it was? Her shinbones screamed. Sweat ran down between her shoulder blades. She had stopped worrying what she would say when she got to Derryward. She wanted only not to be walking any more. She pulled off her cardigan and stuffed it into her satchel and pulled out her blouse from the waistband of her skirt to let the air in. She wished she could take off her shoes and stockings and walk barefoot. But the road was so stony, and there weren't proper grass verges, so that would be even less comfortable.

There were no more cottages, just fields and fields and dry-stone walls on either side. Maybe she could dive behind one of them and go to the lavatory? There was nobody in sight. She decided she could. The relief was immense.

And now, at last, she reached the steep, rutted farm lane. She hoisted her bag up on her shoulder and started up it. The lambs in the fields were bigger now than at Easter. Instead of huddling with their mothers, they were grazing and sporting in little groups, like children in a playground. They broke off their grazing when she walked past and ran back to their mothers, bleating in panic, kicking up their legs. Despite herself she smiled. Then she turned a corner – and there it was. Derryward, its white-washed front shining in the sunlight, the red-painted door half-open as always. A kitten – she thought it was the one she had cuddled at Easter – jumped down off the gate-post when she saw Helen, and re-established herself in a corner of the wall, cleaning her face.

She had thought, last time she left here, that she would never be able to come back. And now here she was, walking up the path as bold as brass.

Let Aunt Bridie be the first person I see, she thought. *Even though she was the one who told us to leave at Easter. Let me be able to explain to her.*

She looked round the yard. There was no sign of Gerry's bicycle against the shed wall. And Fly wasn't about, which probably meant Uncle Sean was out in the fields somewhere. *Good.*

She pushed open the front door. The tiny front hall was dark. She called into the kitchen.

'Um. Hello? Aunt Bridie?'

Her voice felt rusty and unused, her throat scratchy and dry. In a minute Aunt Bridie would appear, perhaps from the scullery at the back. She would be shocked to see Helen – but she would give her a cup of tea and surely, *surely,* she would appreciate the effort Helen had made? Maybe that would cancel out how wrong she had been in the first place. In a few minutes she would be reading the letter and deciding what to do, and it wouldn't be Helen's responsibility any more.

'Hello?' she cried again.

'Who is it?' called a voice from the scullery.

It didn't sound like Aunt Bridie.

'Me. Um – Helen?'

'What on earth are you doing here?'

It wasn't Aunt Bridie. It was Nora, wiping her hands on her striped green pinny. And she didn't look the tiniest bit happy to see Helen.

28.

Helen swallowed, her throat drier than ever, and any faint hope that she might be forgiven for Good Friday died.

Nora's eyes snapped. 'What are you doing here?' she repeated. 'How did you –?' She looked beyond Helen as if searching for her parents.

'I came on my own,' Helen said and, miserable though she was, she couldn't help feeling proud. For the first time in ages she remembered blowing out her birthday candles in this very house, and wishing to be more grown-up. *Well, I am now,* she thought. 'On the train,' she added unnecessarily, for what other way could she have travelled?

'But *why*?' Nora's face suddenly clouded. 'Oh no – is it Michael?' Her round pink cheeks lost their colour.

You see, Michael? Helen thought. *They do still care about you.* If only there was a magical way to tell him this instantly. Wherever he was.

'Yes. No,' Helen said. 'He's fine. At least, he was this morning. But I have come because of him.'

She was so aware of the letter in her satchel that she could hardly believe Nora couldn't see through the leather to the creamy-beige envelope and the neat black handwriting.

But *could* she give it to Nora first? Nora already disliked her so much. Goodness only knew what she would do when she realised the extent of Helen's treachery.

She swallowed. 'I need to see Aunt Bridie,' she said.

Aunt Bridie wouldn't be pleased with what she had done – nobody could be. But she wouldn't fly at her and tear out her hair. She wouldn't tell Helen she hated her. She wouldn't call her names and say she was a baby and a traitor. Even though, Helen thought miserably, she was both of those things.

'Mammy's not here,' Nora said. 'She's away to help lay out Gerry's mother.'

'Lay out?'

'She died this morning,' Nora said. 'Mammy went away up when Gerry came for her. God love him,' she said. 'I wanted to go and help, but Mammy wouldn't let me.' Helen bit her lip, and couldn't help looking at Nora with a new respect. 'She won't be back for a while. And Daddy's away to get the cattle in. So whatever it is, you'll have to tell me.'

'All right.'

Helen pulled her bag off her shoulder and started to undo the straps. She watched her hands fumble, watched the brown leather flap open and saw her hands rummage inside. For a fluttering panicky moment she thought the letter had gone. Could it have fallen out along the road? Or what about on the train, when she was putting *Emma* back in the satchel? But no – there it was. It had worked its way inside *Emma*. She pulled it out, smoothed her hand over the name – which was a bit smudged by now.

'A letter?' Nora snatched the envelope.

Helen chewed her lip. 'Nora,' she said, 'I haven't read this, but – I'm so sorry, but I've had it a while. I was meant to give it to you before and – well, I didn't.'

148

Nora stared at her, her dark eyes wide in disbelief. 'What do you mean you didn't?'

Helen opened her mouth to recite her excuses, and then found herself admitting simply, 'I was angry with you. We had that big fight at Easter and I – well, I just kept it.'

Because I was jealous, she added to herself. *Because it was the one little bit of power I had over you.*

There was no way to say any of that that didn't make her sound like the meanest girl in the world. She wished she could run away while Nora read it – back down the lane, and up the long, long road to the station and all the way home again, but she couldn't. For a start there wasn't another train for hours, and more importantly she needed to see this through.

Nora lifted down a letter-knife from behind the clock on the mantelpiece – *Funny,* Helen thought idly, *they keep their letter-knife in exactly the same place we do* – and slit the envelope open.

Helen didn't want to watch her reading it, but she couldn't bear to look away.

Nora's dark eyes darted left to right, her hands gripping the single sheet tightly.

'When did he send this?' she demanded.

Helen tried to think. 'Um – about six weeks ago, I think,' she whispered. Then she found her courage. 'And I'm so, so sorry, but that's not the important thing now.'

'Who are you to tell me what the important thing is about my own brother?'

'Because you – you don't know the whole story,' Helen said. 'He's been – they sent him to – to Dublin.' She watched Nora's face as she slowly seemed to take in what Helen was saying. 'Do you understand? The riots – I mean, the rebellion – the rising' – gosh, what name would offend Nora least? 'Michael was in the British forces sent to keep order.'

Nora's mouth hung open in shock.

'He *hated* it, Nora. I've never seen anyone so – so ...' She couldn't think of the words to explain the exact nature of how upset Michael was, partly because she didn't understand it. He must have felt a bit like Sandy, she realised. When Private C was shot. She didn't mention the young boy Michael had killed. That was for him to tell – if he ever did

'You've *seen* him? Where?'

Helen shook her head. 'He came home – I mean to Belfast – last night. On embarkation leave. He's meant to go to France on Tuesday. But he says he isn't going. He says he's going to desert.'

Nora gasped. '*My* brother wouldn't do that!' she said, and then she added, 'But he shouldn't be in the British army in the first place.' She bent over, hugging herself. 'Oh God!' Her voice was despairing. 'It's all so *complicated*! And you – you've made it a million times worse.'

'I know,' Helen said in a tiny voice. 'But Nora – he *mustn't* desert. They'll track him down and shoot him. That's what happens.'

'Ha!' Nora said. 'Well, the Brits have proved they can do plenty of shooting.' She shook her head. 'But they'd hardly bother with Michael, surely.'

'They *would*,' Helen insisted. 'Look,' she said,

remembering the newspaper stories she had forced herself to read, 'at how many rebels – um, patriots, they've taken prisoner. A *thousand*. And maybe Michael's only one soldier, but they make examples of deserters. Because of morale, and not encouraging others. And Michael doesn't have a clue where to go, or where to hide.'

Nora wiped her hands on her pinny again, though they must have been perfectly dry.

'I don't think he *wants* to desert, really,' Helen added in a sudden burst of insight. 'I think he needs you – all of you – to tell him he's still welcome here. That he has somewhere to come home to.' She ran out of words and breath and had to stop for a moment.

Nora was still staring at her, unspeaking.

'He ran off this morning,' Helen went on, 'when I told him I hadn't given you the letter. I've never seen anyone so angry – not even you. *That's* why I'm here – because I need you to get the next train back to Belfast and help me find him – he's bound to come back to my house eventually. *Me* telling him won't be enough – I don't suppose he trusts me any more. *You* have to tell him you understand that he did what he had to do.'

'But I don't!' Nora cried. She was shaking her head slowly. Even her lips were white, as if she was in shock. 'Michael's my brother, but – but I don't understand how he could have fought against patriots. *Against Ireland.*' Her voice shook. 'So no,' she said. 'I – I can't help.'

She went to turn away, but Helen grabbed her elbow, and said, in horror, 'Nora! Surely all that – about patriots and Ireland – isn't as important as *family*?'

But though the tears stood in Nora's eyes, her lips were set in a firm line. 'It is to me,' she said. 'The leaders who were shot this week – they have families too. It didn't stop them doing what they believed in.'

With a gulp, she pulled away from Helen's grasp, ran out of the room and up the stairs. Helen heard her bedroom door bang.

Helen stood helplessly in the kitchen. *I don't know what to do now,* she thought. *I can't just go home.* Then she thought, *Yes, I do know. I'll have to show the letter to Uncle Sean. He's the only one left.*

Her stomach dipped at the very idea of confessing to Uncle Sean. She remembered the purple bruise Michael had sported when he had first run away; the way Uncle Sean and Papa had squared up to each other at Easter. But he wouldn't hit *her,* would he?

Well, even if he did, she had to be brave. She wasn't 'wee Helen' any more and she couldn't go round acting like her. So she took the letter, put it back into her satchel, slung the satchel over her shoulder and went back outside. The spring evening was cooling now, the shadows lengthening in the kitchen garden. Uncle Sean must be in the milking parlour because Fly lay across the door, head on her paws, tongue lolling. She gave Helen a polite wriggle of her backside as she passed, but didn't go as far as wagging her tail. Helen had always hated the milking parlour – the thick smell of the cows, and the stink of milk, and the cows' big mucky bottoms all turned towards her in a very alarming way, but today she hardly noticed.

Uncle Sean was near the far end of the row of cows, bending down. He didn't notice Helen come in and she stood for a moment, noticing how alone he seemed in the parlour. *He must miss Michael,* she thought, *as much as we miss Sandy. More.*

'Uncle Sean?' she said.

He was even more shocked to see her than Nora and, like Nora's, his eyes narrowed in suspicion. 'Who brought you?' he demanded.

'I came on my own. I had to show you' – she scrabbled for the letter – 'this.'

Uncle Sean read the letter much more slowly than Nora, and when he had finished he turned to Helen.

'Daughter?' he asked. 'Why did you not show us this before?'

Tears flooded her eyes. She couldn't say what she had said to Nora – that she had been angry.

All she could say was, 'I don't know. I tried. I'm so sorry. But – Uncle Sean' – her stomach dipped – 'there's more.'

Uncle Sean's big red face whitened. His lips moved without forming words. 'Oh, God,' he said. 'Don't tell me, daughter.'

And Helen realised that he thought she had come to tell him his son was dead.

'*No!*' she said, and, surprised at herself, she placed a reassuring hand on his tweed-clad arm. 'He's all right. At least –'

She told him. She emphasised that Michael had had no choice, that he would never have chosen to go to Dublin.

'And now he plans to desert,' she finished, 'because he feels so bad about being involved. He's ashamed.'

Uncle Sean shook his head. 'I'm ashamed of him too,' he admitted. He pulled at the cow's udder for a while. Helen heard the rasp of his breath. Then he said, 'But – proud too. That he went through with what he thought was right. Even though I think it was wrong. Och, that doesn't make sense, does it? Feeling two things at the same time?'

'I spend half my life feeling two different things,' Helen admitted. 'Never knowing what I'm meant to believe in. What side I'm meant to be on. Maybe that's why I could understand what it was like for Michael – that feeling of being torn.'

How strange that she could tell this to Uncle Sean of all people. When it didn't make sense inside her own head, and she couldn't explain it properly to people like Miss Cassidy and George, people who were clever and broad-minded. She had never thought of Uncle Sean as being either. And yet he nodded with understanding.

'I wouldn't want my son to be a quitter,' he said. 'He wasn't raised to give up on things. And I couldn't bear to think of him going on the run, being hunted down like a fox and shot by the army. I'd rather – well, I'd rather he died fighting. Even for the British.'

'*That's* what he needs to hear,' Helen said. Tiredness swamped her. 'But how can he?' she wailed. 'I don't even know where he is.' She told Uncle Sean what had happened that morning. 'I didn't know how much he cared about all of you,' she said, 'until then.'

Uncle Sean slapped the cow on her brown rump.

'Aye,' he said, so softly that Helen hardly heard him. 'Your principles are important, but not as important as your family.'

It was the opposite of what Nora had said, and Uncle Sean said it with an air of surprise, as if he had just realised it himself. For a long time there was silence in the milking parlour, only the shifting and lowing of the cattle.

And then a new sound as Fly suddenly jumped up and started to bark. The cattle looked round in alarm, and Uncle Sean swore under his breath.

'Whisht, Fly,' he called. 'Settle yourself.'

But Fly didn't settle herself. Tail whirling, she ran out into the yard, barking at the top of her voice. She came back in, a few seconds later, dancing and leaping, and after her, his kit bag over his shoulder, his cap in his hand as if, like her, he had found the long walk from the station too hot, came Michael.

When Uncle Sean saw him his hands dropped to his sides, and hung there as if he didn't know what to do with them. And then he lifted them, and clapped Michael on the back, and said, 'Och, son. You're home.'

29.

Michael and Helen leaned over the wall and looked across the valley. The field bottoms were hidden by a skein of evening mist. Fly sighed and pressed herself against Michael's legs.

'I can't bear to leave it again,' Michael said. 'I can't believe I was so keen to go.'

'But you *are* leaving? You're not deserting?'

He nodded. 'I still can't bear to think about Dublin,' he said. 'But I signed up for the duration. And at least – well, I suppose fighting the Germans I know what I'm fighting *for*. All this.' He waved an arm to take in the green and grey hills and the dark hunched shadow of the Mournes. 'And I'll be fighting to get back here safe.'

They were both silent. Helen felt the rough cool stone under her hand.

'Today,' Michael went on, 'I felt so lost. I wandered the streets for hours. I didn't know where I was. All that red brick! And then I found my way back to your house. It was the only place I could think of. And your da had been to get you from Mabel's house, but there was nobody there. They didn't know where you'd got to. They were frantic. Uncle James kept saying you weren't the type to run away – it made me feel so ashamed. Because I didn't think *I* was. And then they went up to your room and saw the note. *They* didn't know what it meant – you just said you were going to deliver the letter. But I knew you must have come here. And so – well, I got the next train.

Your mammy wasn't fit to come and your da wouldn't leave her.'

'Is Mama all right?' Helen asked fearfully. All her life she had been brought up not to worry her mother.

'I think so. She just wasn't fit for that long journey on top of worrying about you.'

'It *was* long.'

Helen was very relieved not to be making the journey again until Monday night, when she would travel back to Belfast with Michael. She would see him off to the Front, as she had seen Sandy off. She would have to miss a day of school but she would work hard to make up for it. Somehow she felt like working hard now. And she *was* going to join the scholarship class no matter what Mama said. However uncertain she felt about – well, about so many things, surely learning how to think properly could only help her know who she was and what she believed in.

'Were you not scared?' Michael asked, and Helen, lost in a dream of college, blinked, then realised he was asking about her lone train journey.

'Yes,' she admitted. 'But I *had* to do it. I had to make up for letting you down. For being "a stupid wee girl".'

'I'm sorry,' Michael said. 'I shouldn't have – I was so angry – I didn't know what I was –'

'It's all right. I had to let your family know how you felt. Even if it was too late.'

'It wasn't too late.'

'No.'

They were silent then, looking over the valley and watching the shadows stretch across the fields. *Soon,*

Helen thought, *the shadow will reach the hedge and then it will be quite dark.*

But before it did, a shadow detached itself from the house wall and, as it grew closer, Helen saw that it was Nora, a shawl pulled round her in the chill of the cloudless evening. She lifted up her head and called up to them, 'Mammy says come in for your suppers.'

Helen expected her to turn and go straight back inside. She had refused to come out of her room to greet her brother even when Aunt Bridie had gone up to beg her.

But now she kept walking towards them, and as they got closer Helen saw that an uncertain smile flickered round her mouth.

Michael looked at Helen. 'We'd better go in,' he said, and they walked down the hill to meet Nora.

THE END